The Legend of

JOHNNY
Appleseed

Graphic Spin is published by Stone Arch Books
A Capstone Imprint
151 Good Counsel Drive, P.O. Box 669
Mankato, Minnesota 56002
www.capstonepub.com

Library of Congress Cataloging-in-Publication Data
Powell, Martin.
   The legend of Johnny Appleseed : the graphic novel retold by Martin Powell ; illustrated
by M.A. Lamoreaux.
   p. cm. -- Graphic spin
   ISBN 978-1-4342-1895-7 library binding -- ISBN 978-1-4342-2266-4 pbk.
   1. Appleseed, Johnny, 1774-1845--Juvenile fiction. 2. Graphic novels. ff1. Graphic novels.
2. Appleseed, Johnny, 1774-1845--Fiction.   I. Lamoreaux, M. A., ill. II. Title.
   PZ7.7.P69Leg 2010
   741.5'973--dc22
                                                                          2009029330

Summary: Little Johnny Appleseed had a big heart, and even bigger dreams. The young
boy hoped to one day spread his love of apples by planting apple seeds across the entire
country. That way, the apples can feed the hungry, and everyone can enjoy the beautiful
trees. So, one day, Johnny sets out to do just that! His adventures bring him face to face
with an injured wolf, a giant catfish, the bigfoot, and much more in this tall tale of a true
American legend.

Art Directors: Bob Lentz and Kay Fraser

Graphic Designer: Emily Harris

Production Specialist: Michelle Biedscheid

Printed in the United States of America
in Stevens Point, Wisconsin.
092009
005619WZS10

The Legend of

JOHNNY
Appleseed

RETOLD BY MARTIN POWELL
ILLUSTRATED BY M.A. LAMOREAUX

STONE ARCH BOOKS
a capstone imprint

Cast of Characters

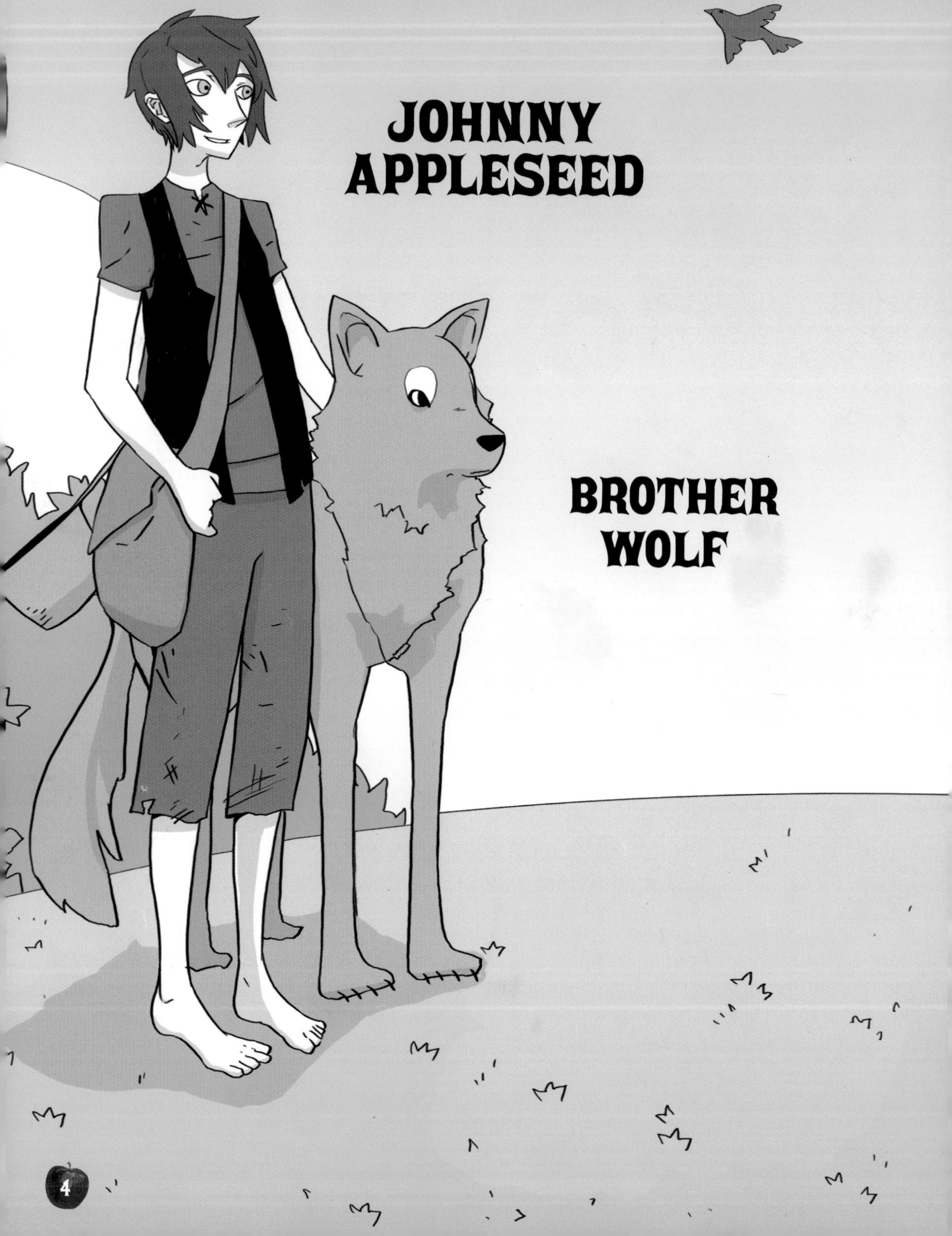
JOHNNY
APPLESEED
BROTHER
WOLF

FRIENDS OF JOHNNY APPLESEED

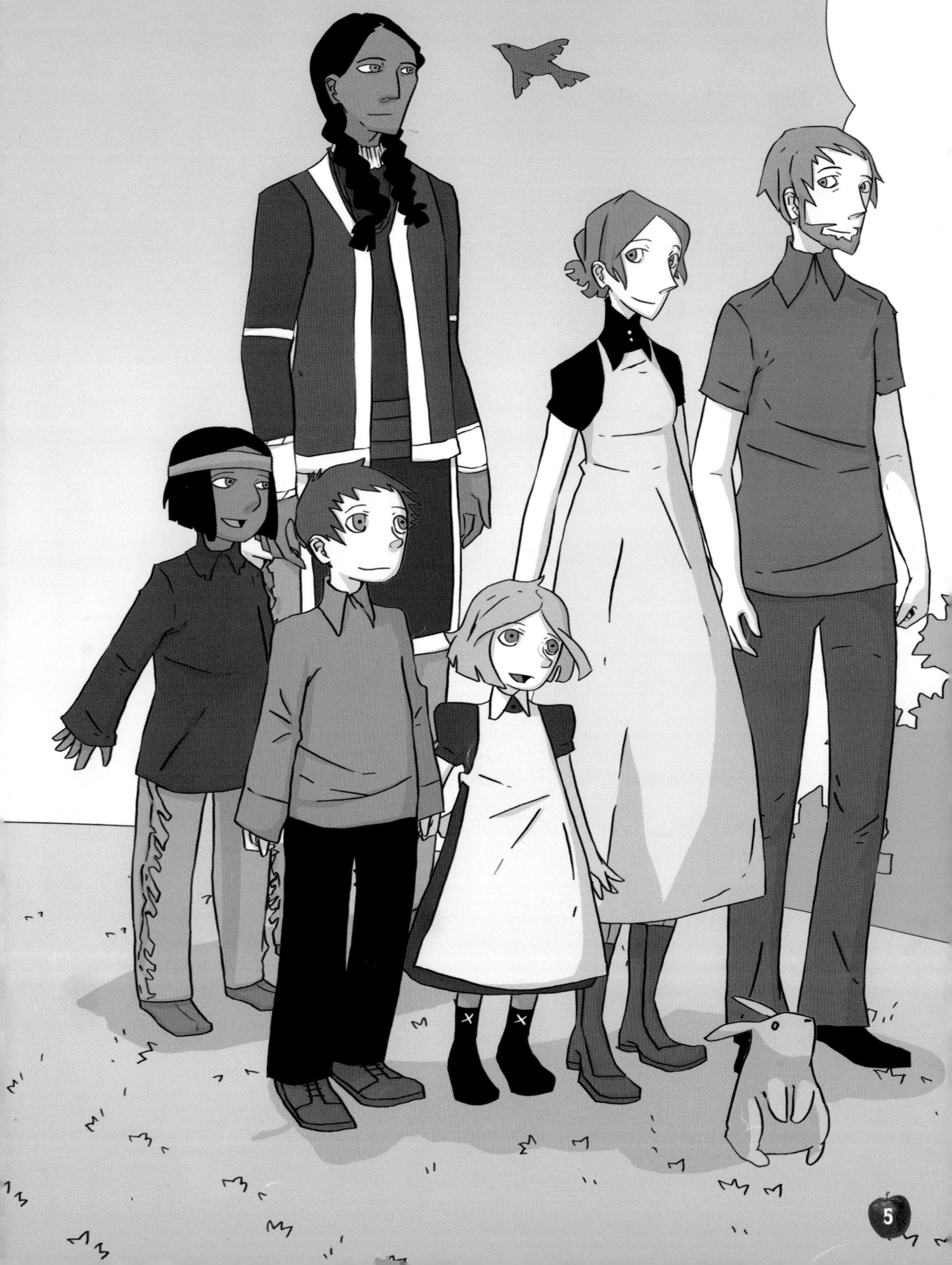

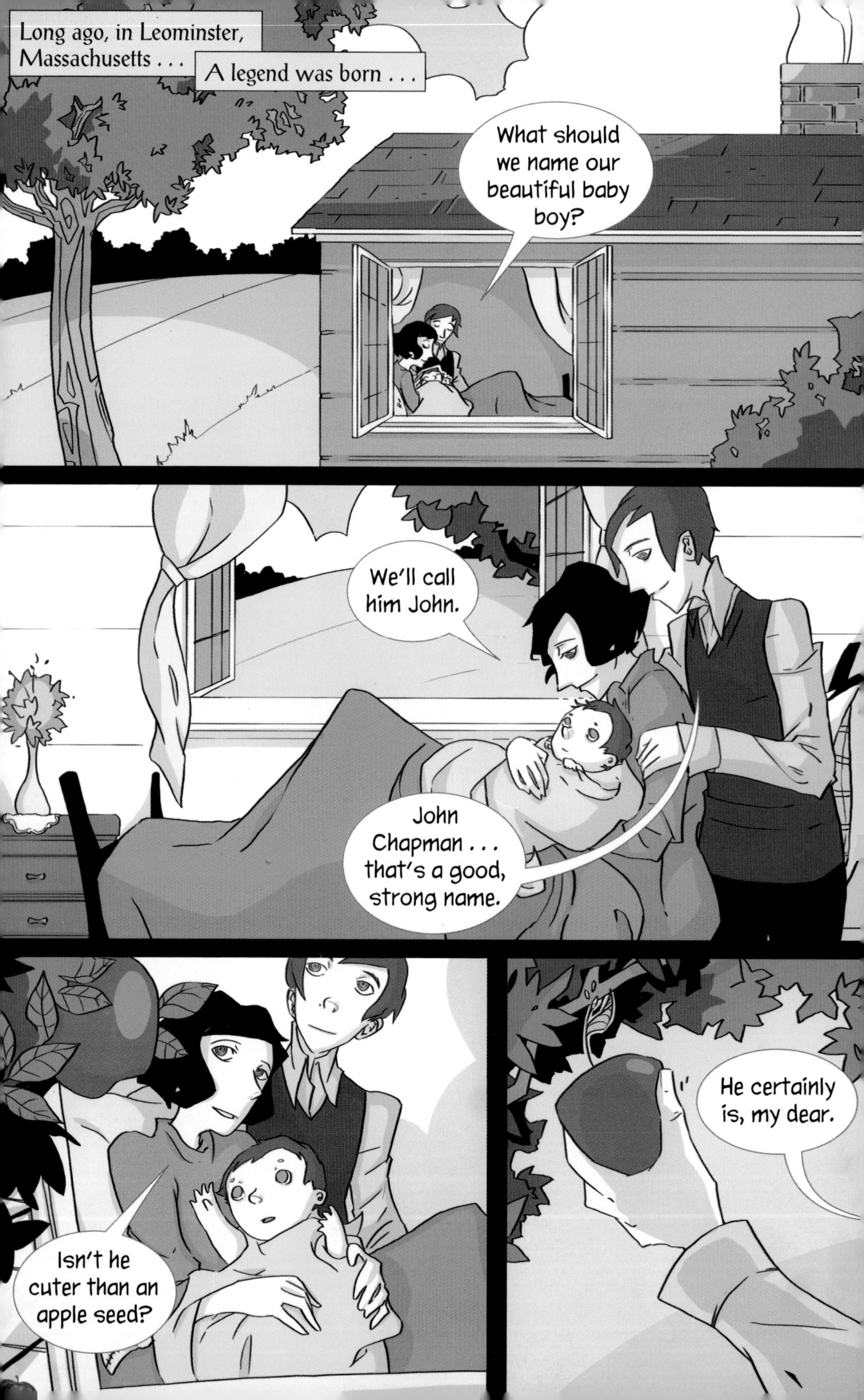
Long ago, in Leominster, Massachusetts . . .
A legend was born . . .
What should we name our beautiful baby boy?
We'll call him John.
John Chapman . . . that's a good, strong name.
Isn't he cuter than an apple seed?
He certainly is, my dear.

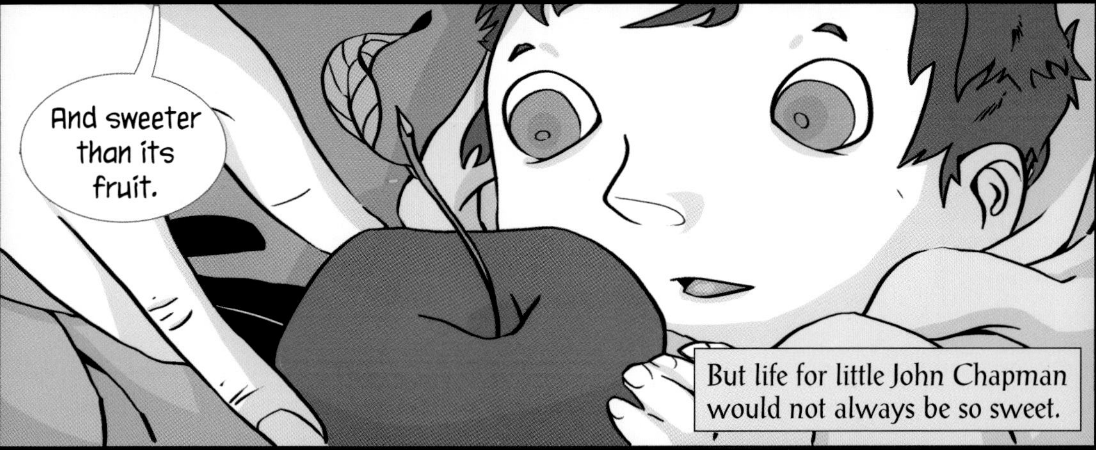
And sweeter than its fruit.
But life for little John Chapman would not always be so sweet.
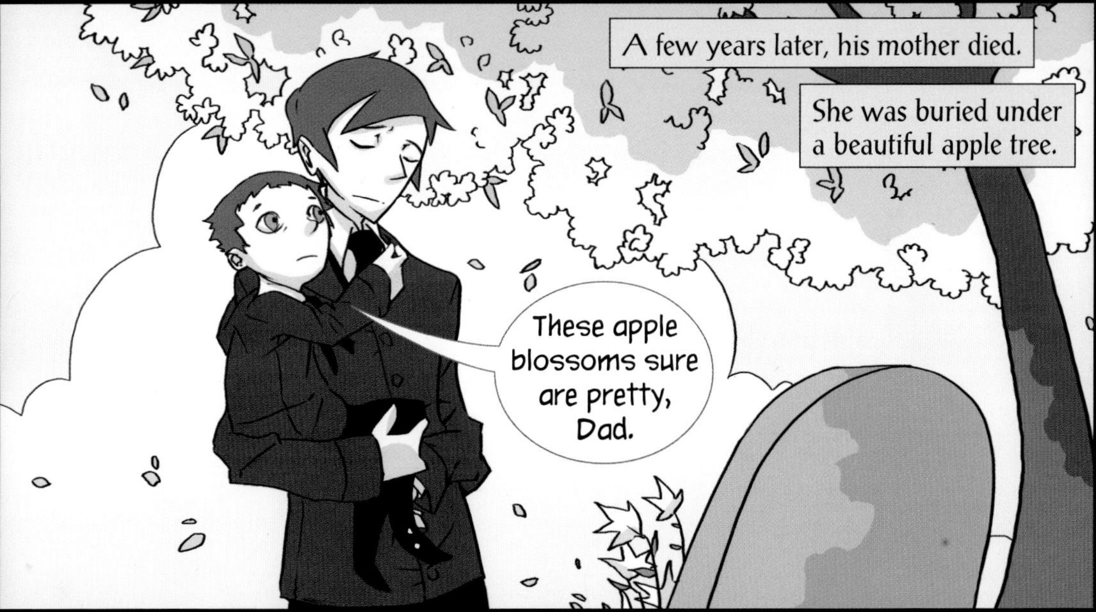
A few years later, his mother died.
She was buried under a beautiful apple tree.
These apple blossoms sure are pretty, Dad.
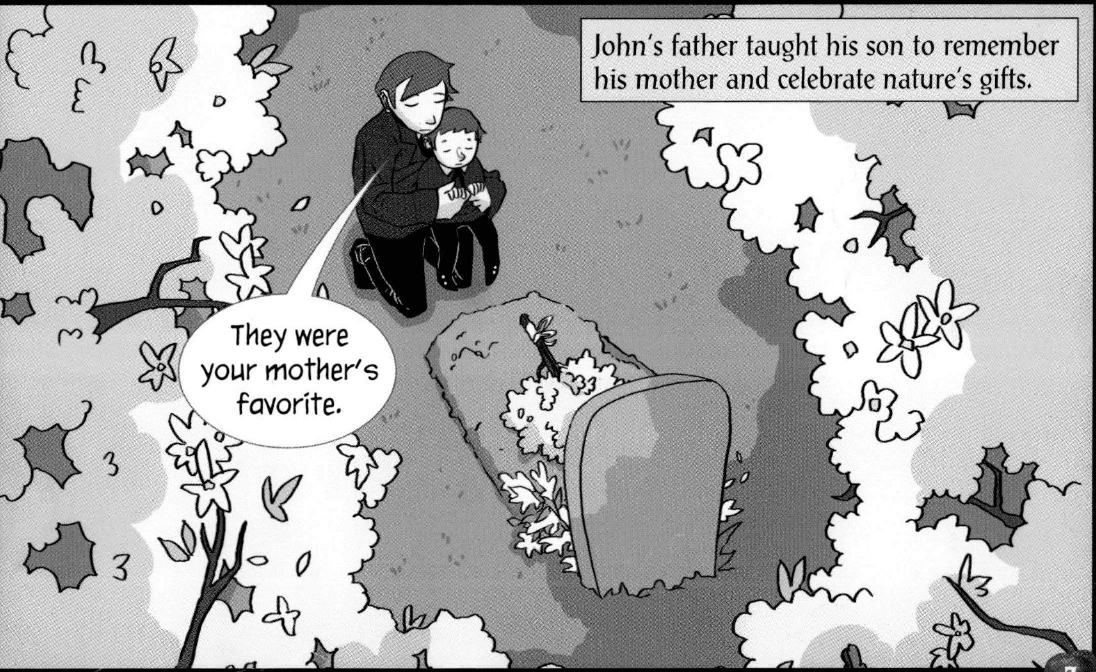
John's father taught his son to remember his mother and celebrate nature's gifts.
They were your mother's favorite.

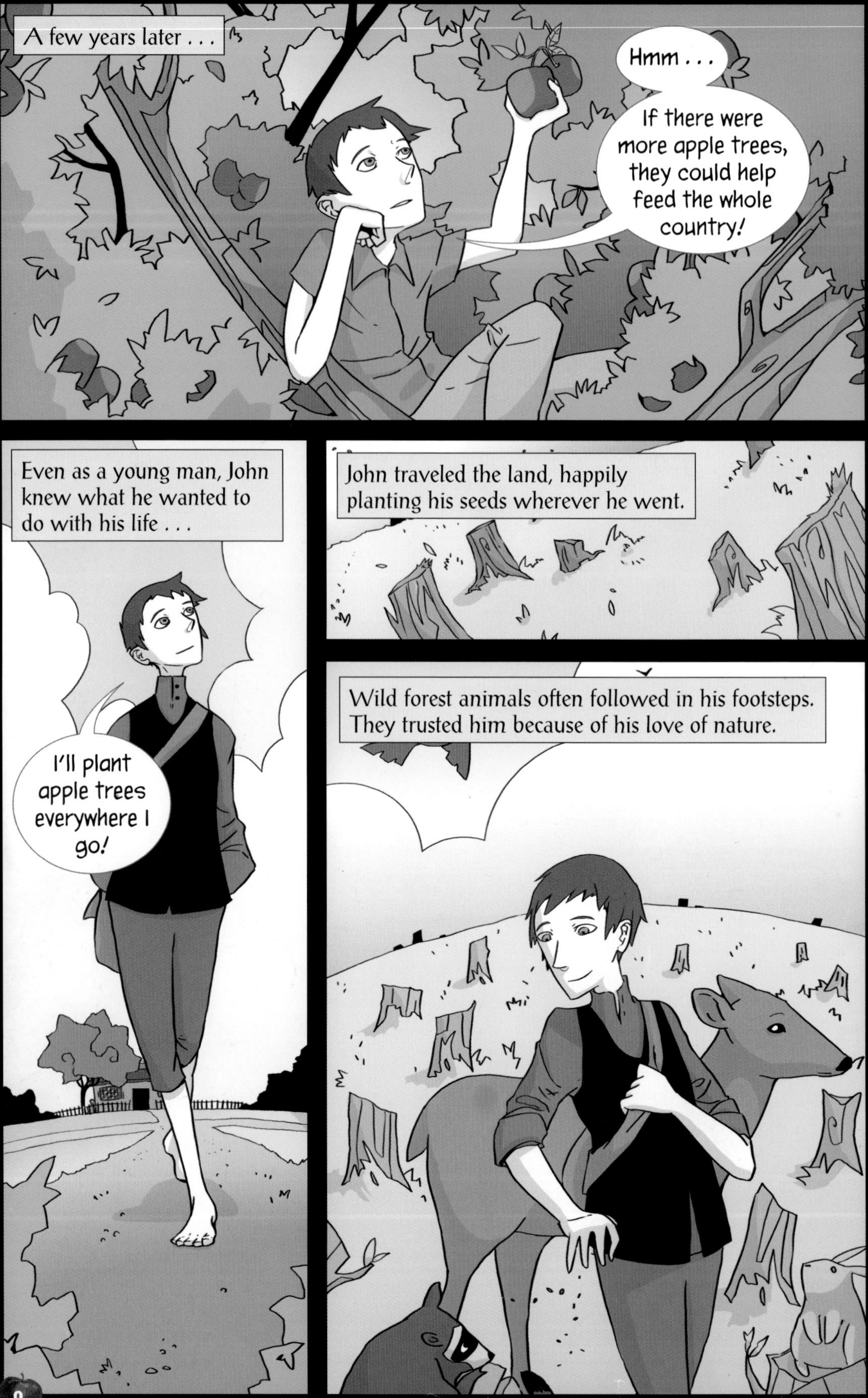
A few years later . . .
Hmm . . .
If there were more apple trees, they could help feed the whole country!
Even as a young man, John knew what he wanted to do with his life . . .
I'll plant apple trees everywhere I go!
John traveled the land, happily planting his seeds wherever he went.
Wild forest animals often followed in his footsteps. They trusted him because of his love of nature.

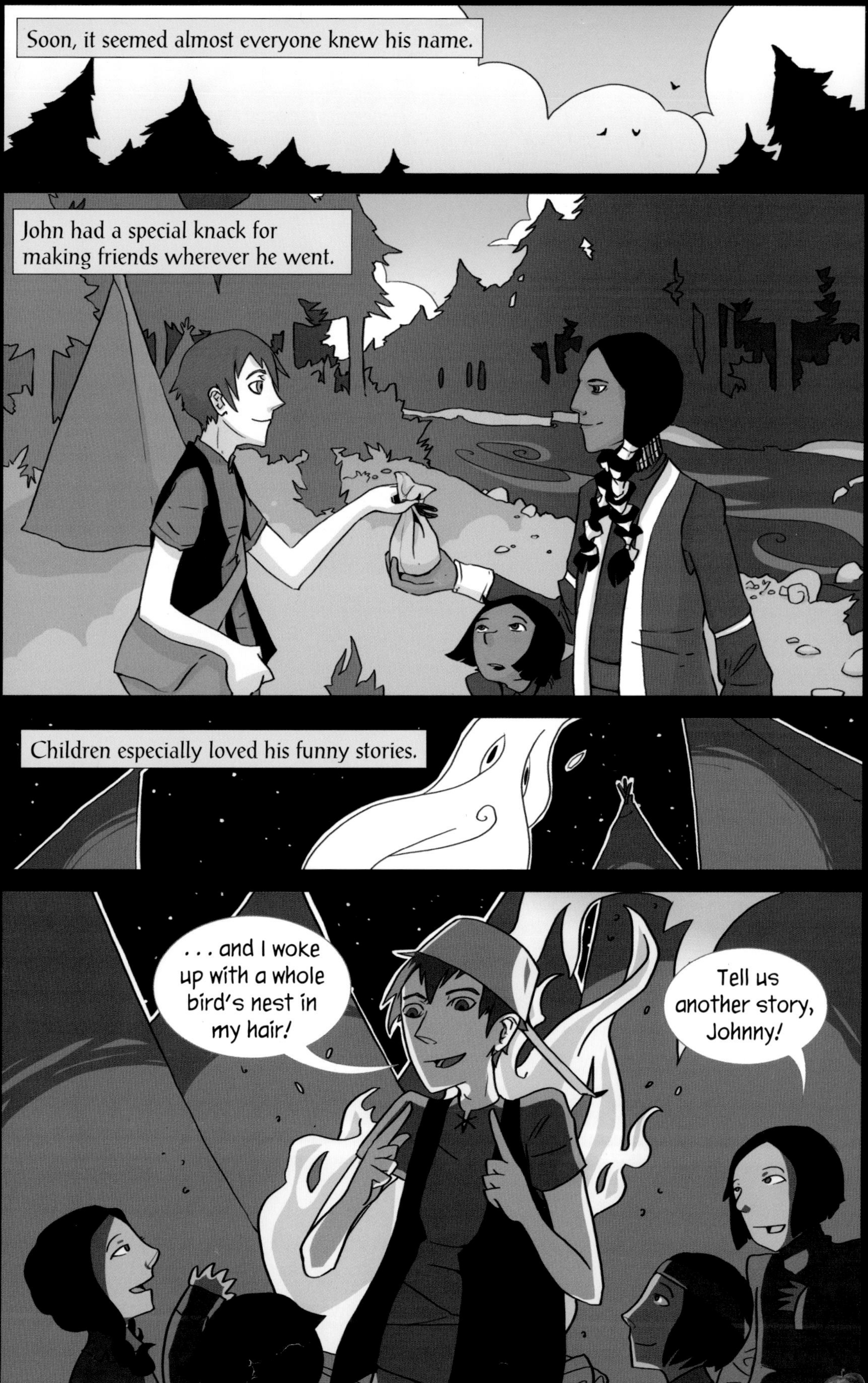
Soon, it seemed almost everyone knew his name.
John had a special knack for making friends wherever he went.
Children especially loved his funny stories.
. . . and I woke up with a whole bird's nest in my hair!
Tell us another story, Johnny!

John's kind heart became as well-known as his tall tales.

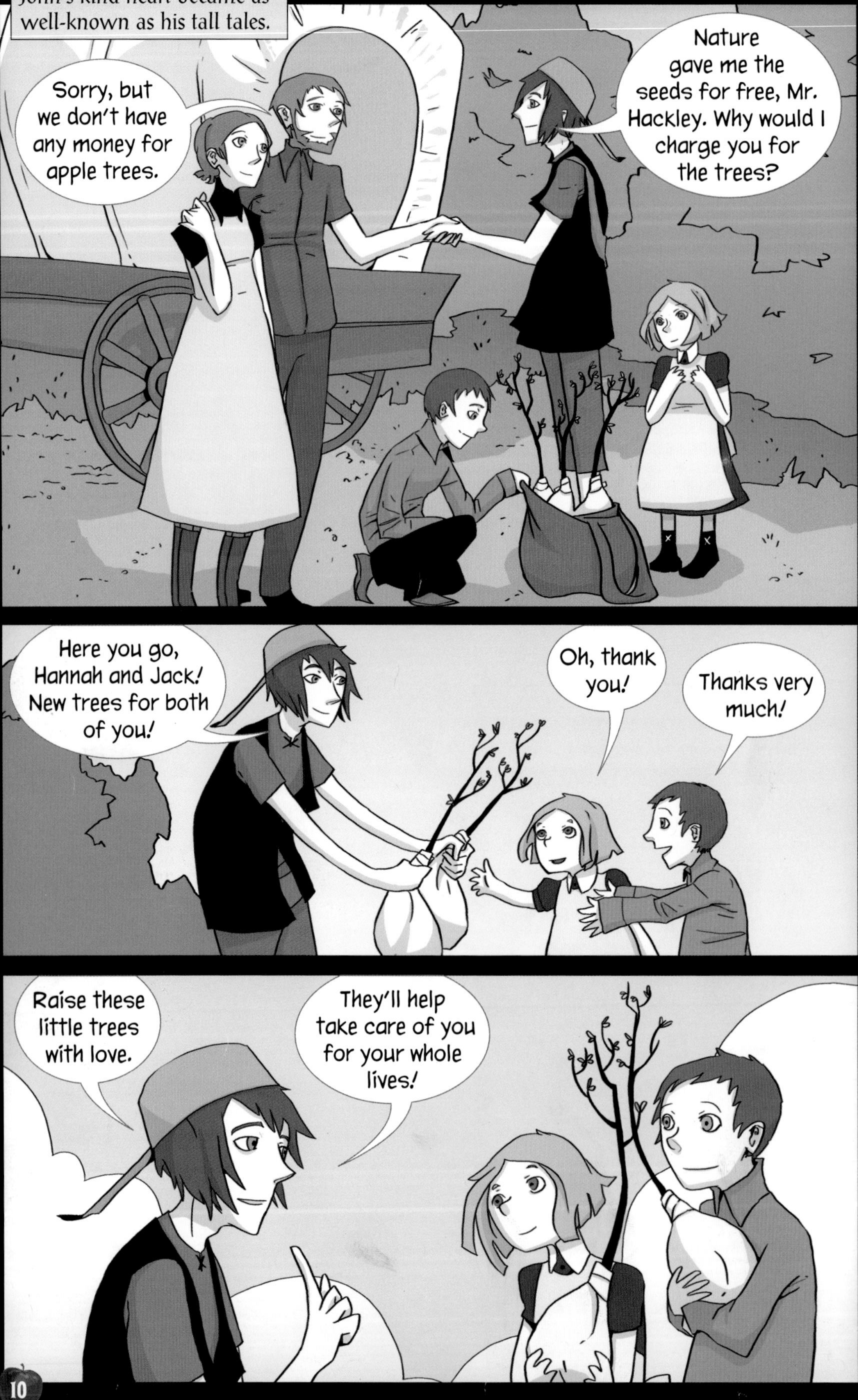
Sorry, but we don't have any money for apple trees.
Nature gave me the seeds for free, Mr. Hackley. Why would I charge you for the trees?
Here you go, Hannah and Jack! New trees for both of you!
Oh, thank you!
Thanks very much!
Raise these little trees with love.
They'll help take care of you for your whole lives!

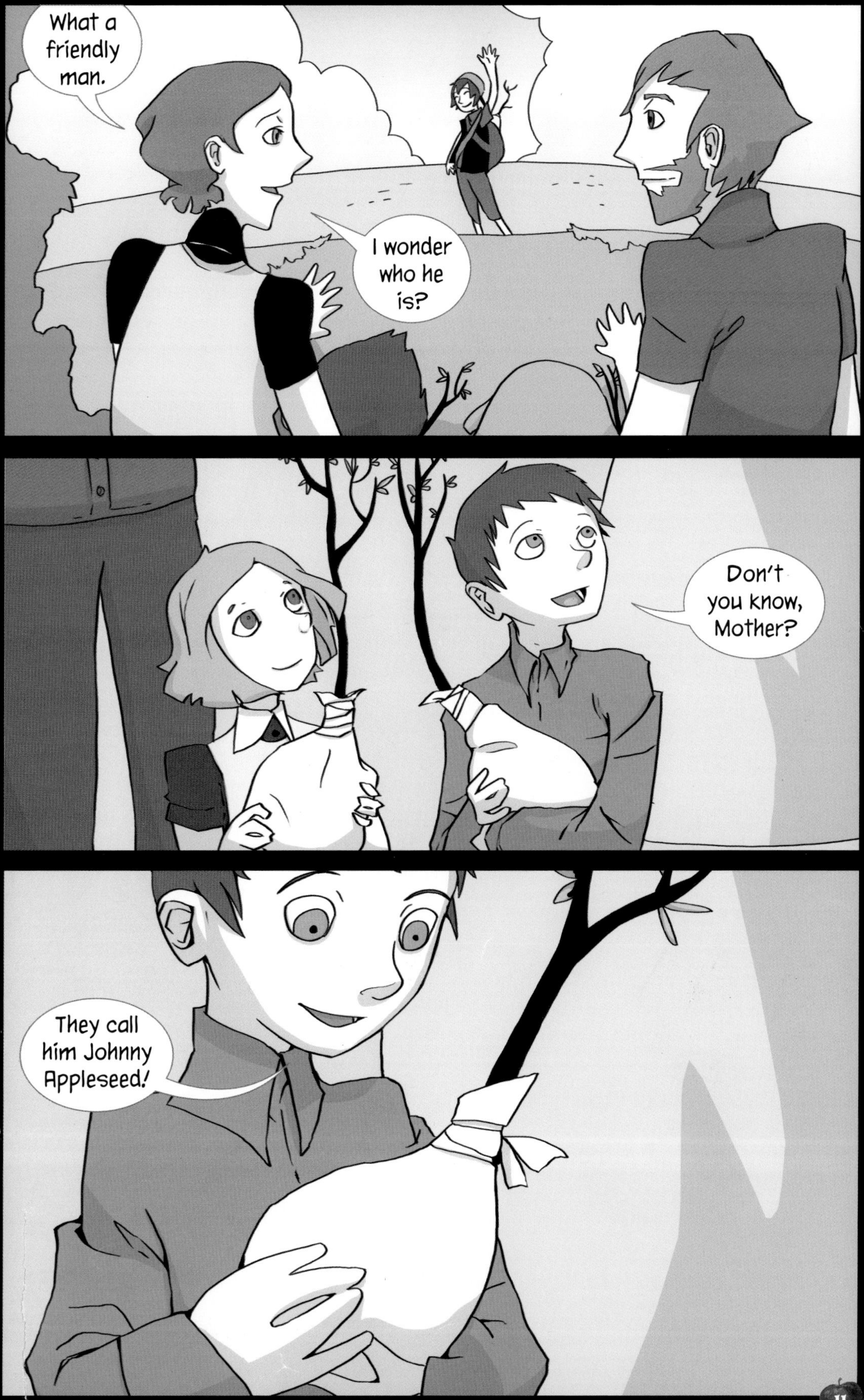
What a friendly man.
I wonder who he is?
Don't you know, Mother?
They call him Johnny Appleseed!

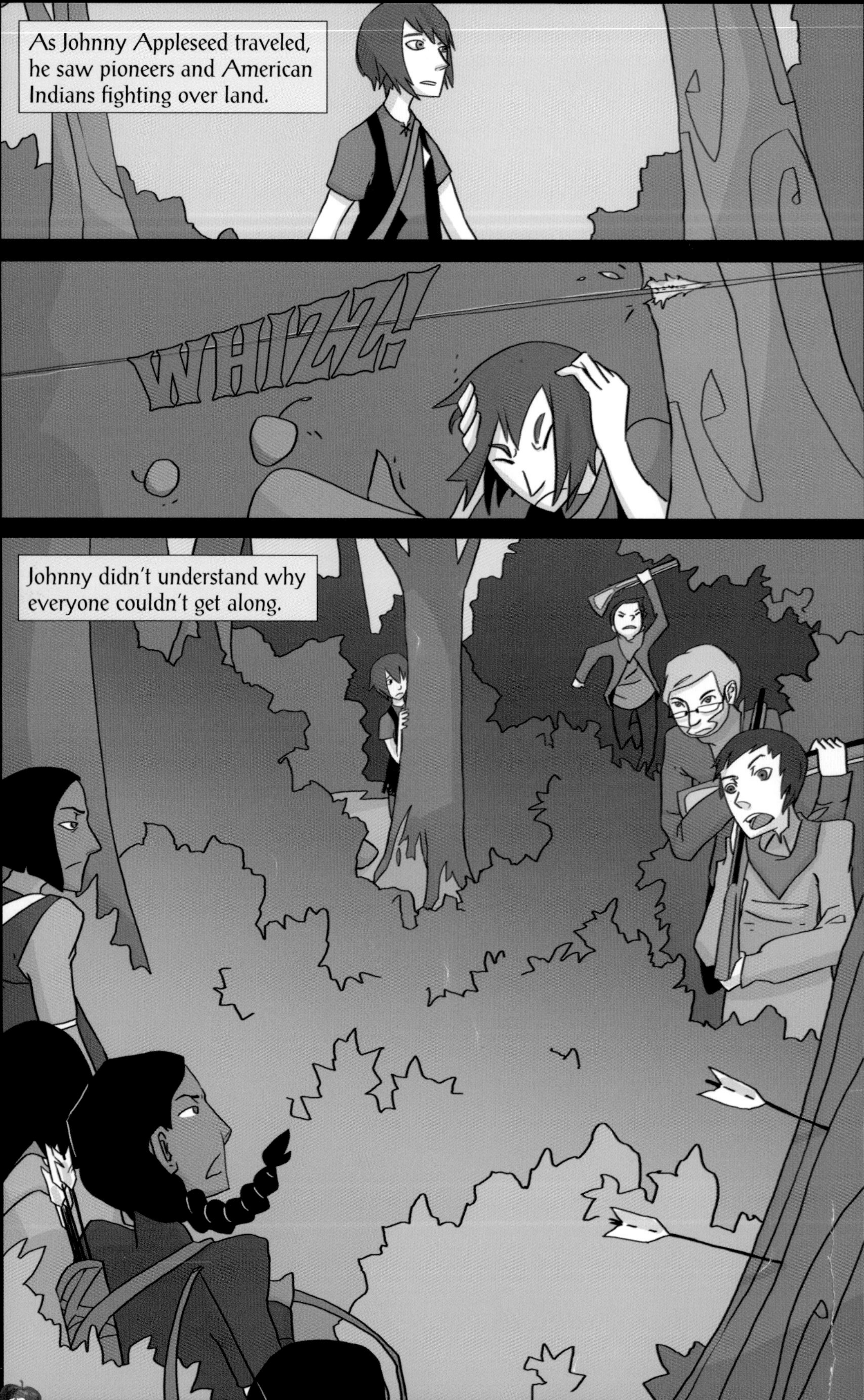
As Johnny Appleseed traveled, he saw pioneers and American Indians fighting over land.
WHIZZ!
Johnny didn't understand why everyone couldn't get along.

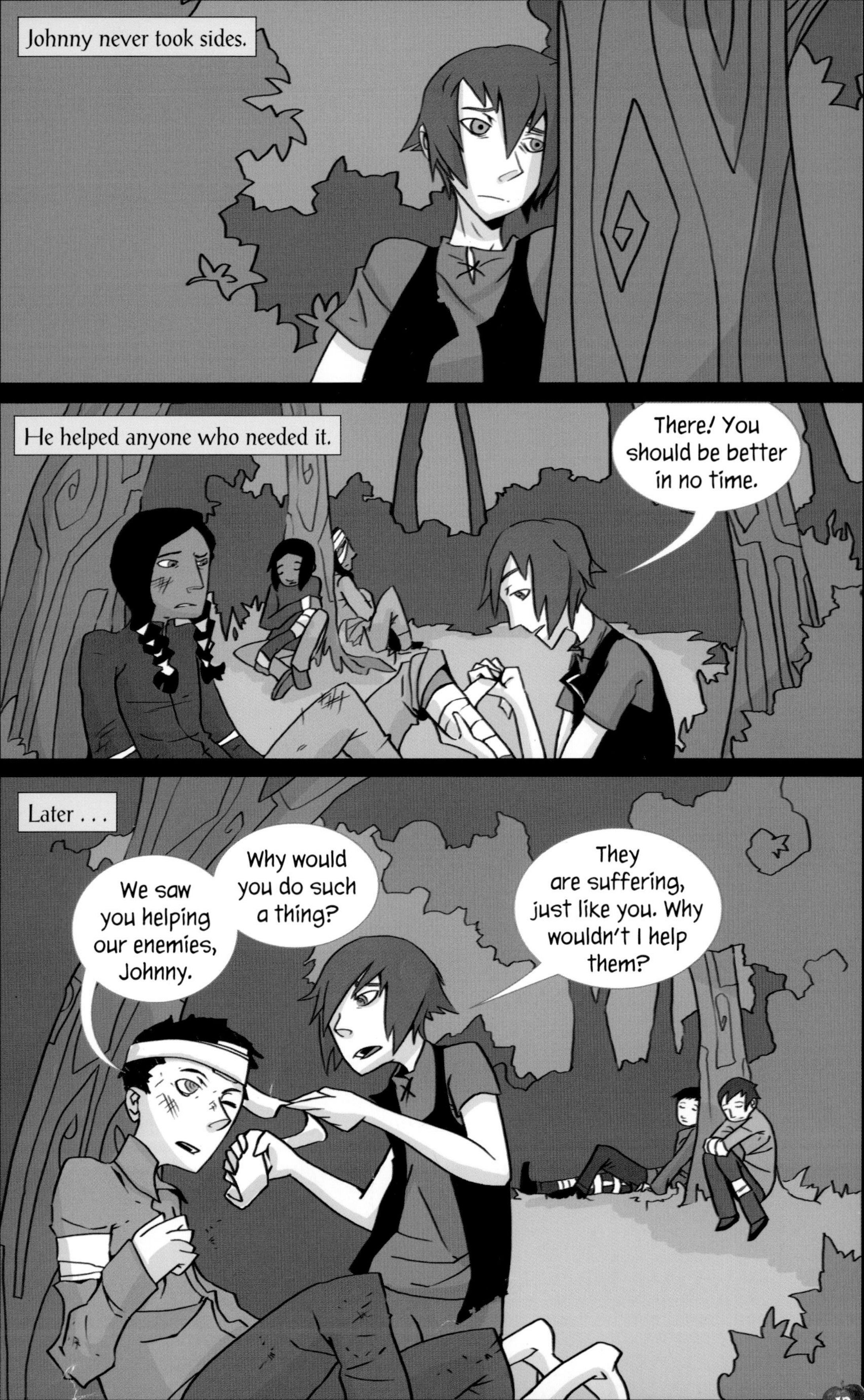
Johnny never took sides.
He helped anyone who needed it.
There! You should be better in no time.
Later . . .
We saw you helping our enemies, Johnny.
Why would you do such a thing?
They are suffering, just like you. Why wouldn't I help them?

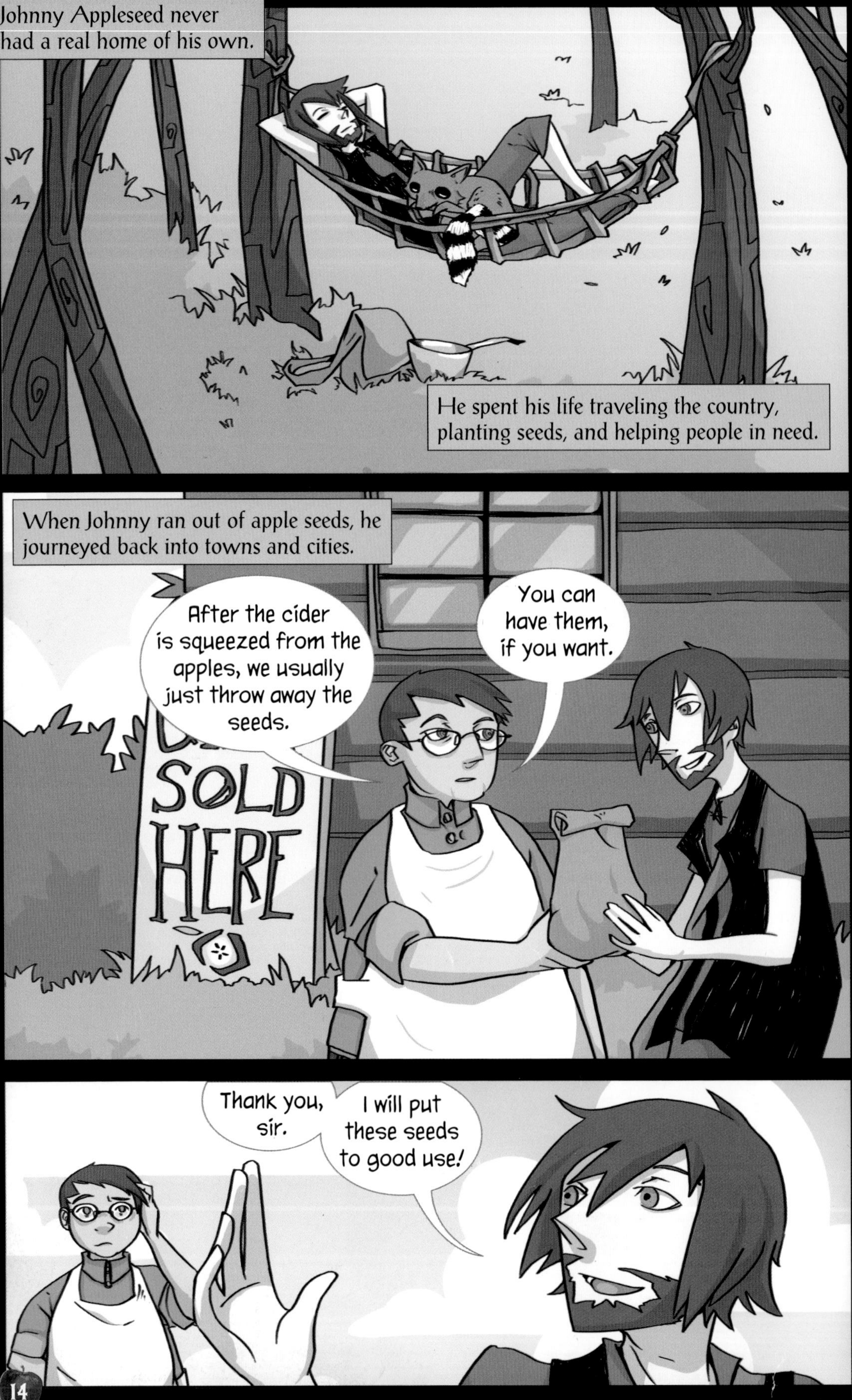
Johnny Appleseed never had a real home of his own.
He spent his life traveling the country, planting seeds, and helping people in need.
When Johnny ran out of apple seeds, he journeyed back into towns and cities.
After the cider is squeezed from the apples, we usually just throw away the seeds.
You can have them, if you want.
SOLD HERE
Thank you, sir.
I will put these seeds to good use!

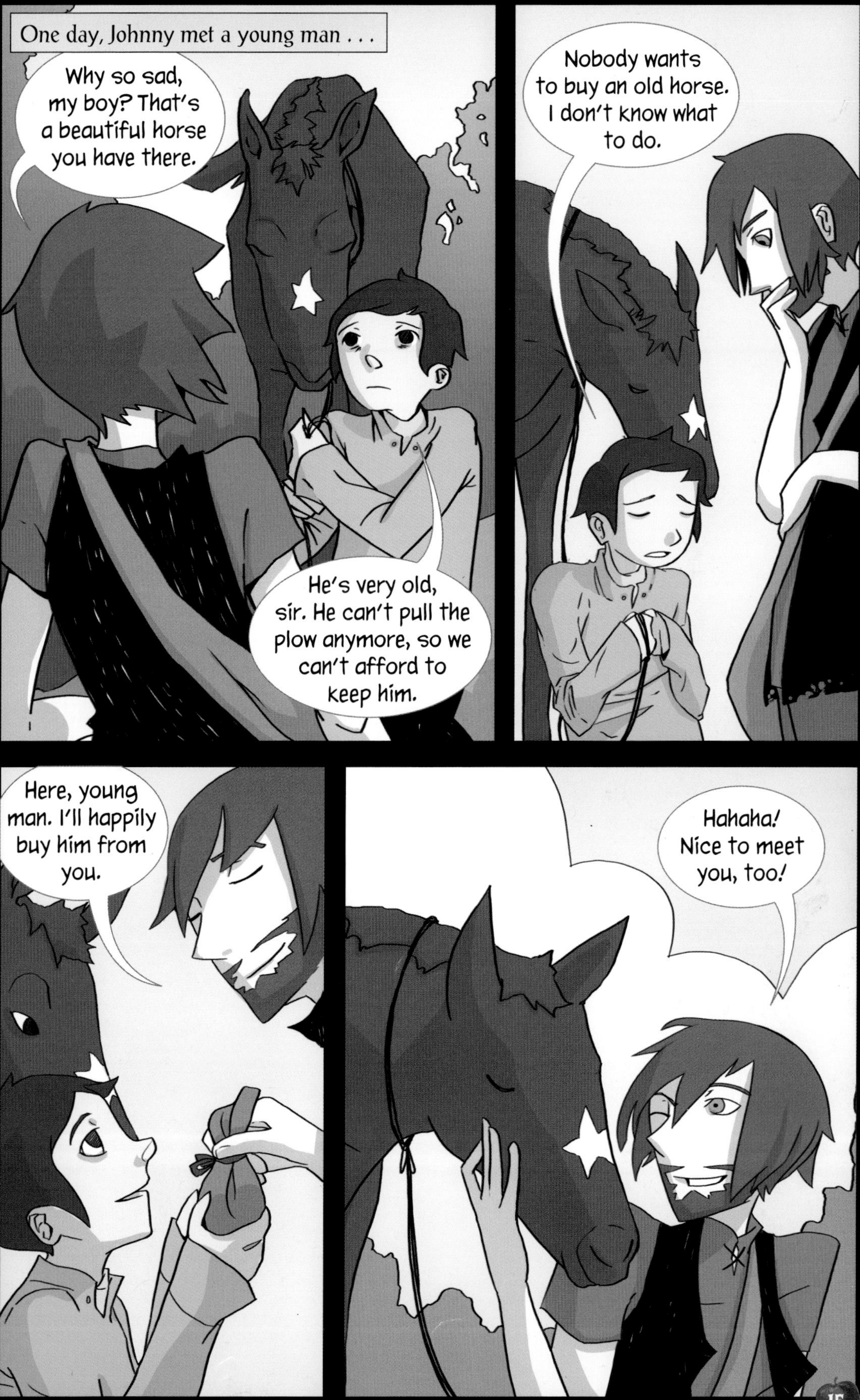

One day, Johnny met a young man . . .
Why so sad, my boy? That's a beautiful horse you have there.
He's very old, sir. He can't pull the plow anymore, so we can't afford to keep him.
Nobody wants to buy an old horse. I don't know what to do.
Here, young man. I'll happily buy him from you.
Hahaha! Nice to meet you, too!

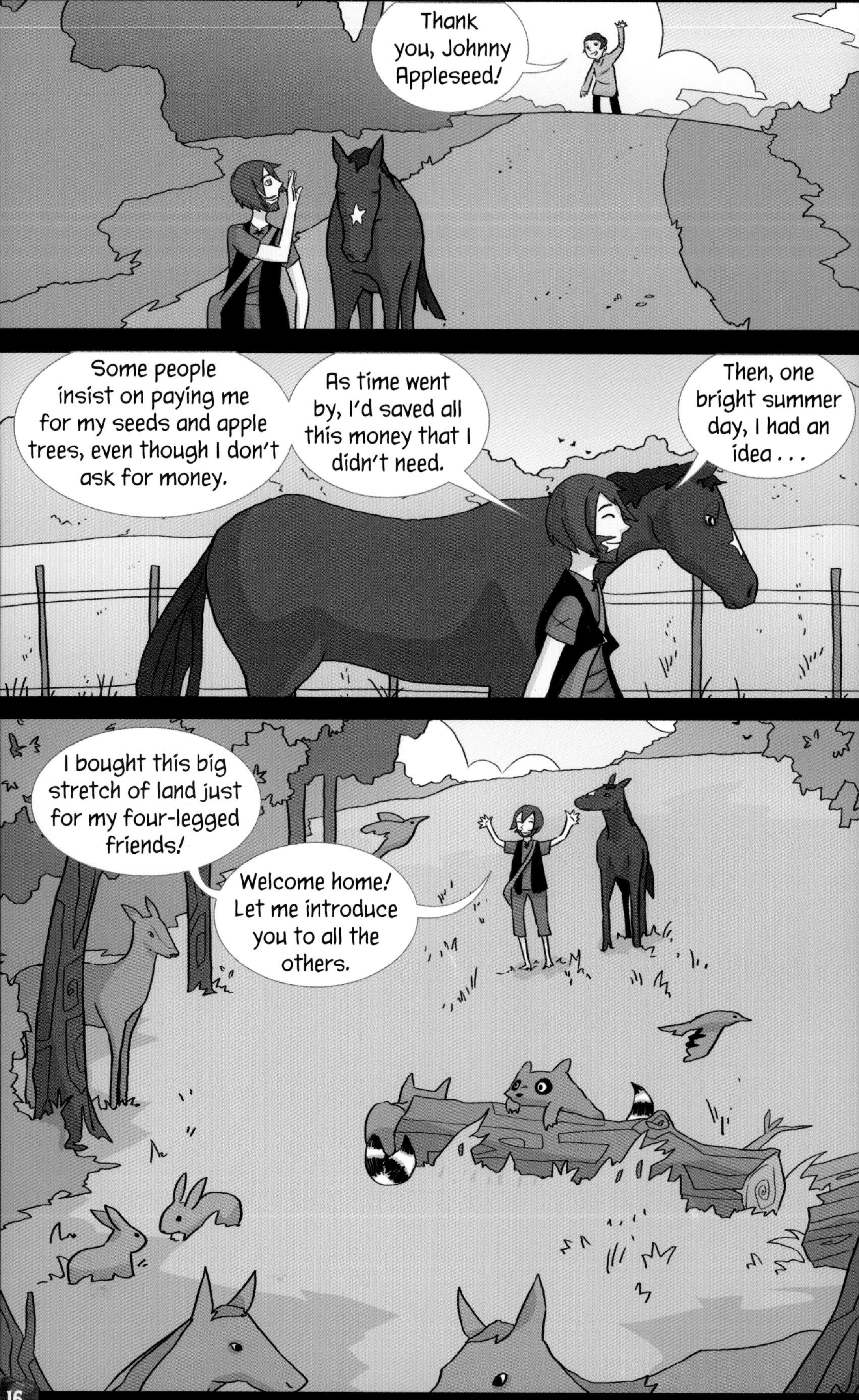
Thank you, Johnny Appleseed!
Some people insist on paying me for my seeds and apple trees, even though I don't ask for money.
As time went by, I'd saved all this money that I didn't need.
Then, one bright summer day, I had an idea . . .
I bought this big stretch of land just for my four-legged friends!
Welcome home! Let me introduce you to all the others.

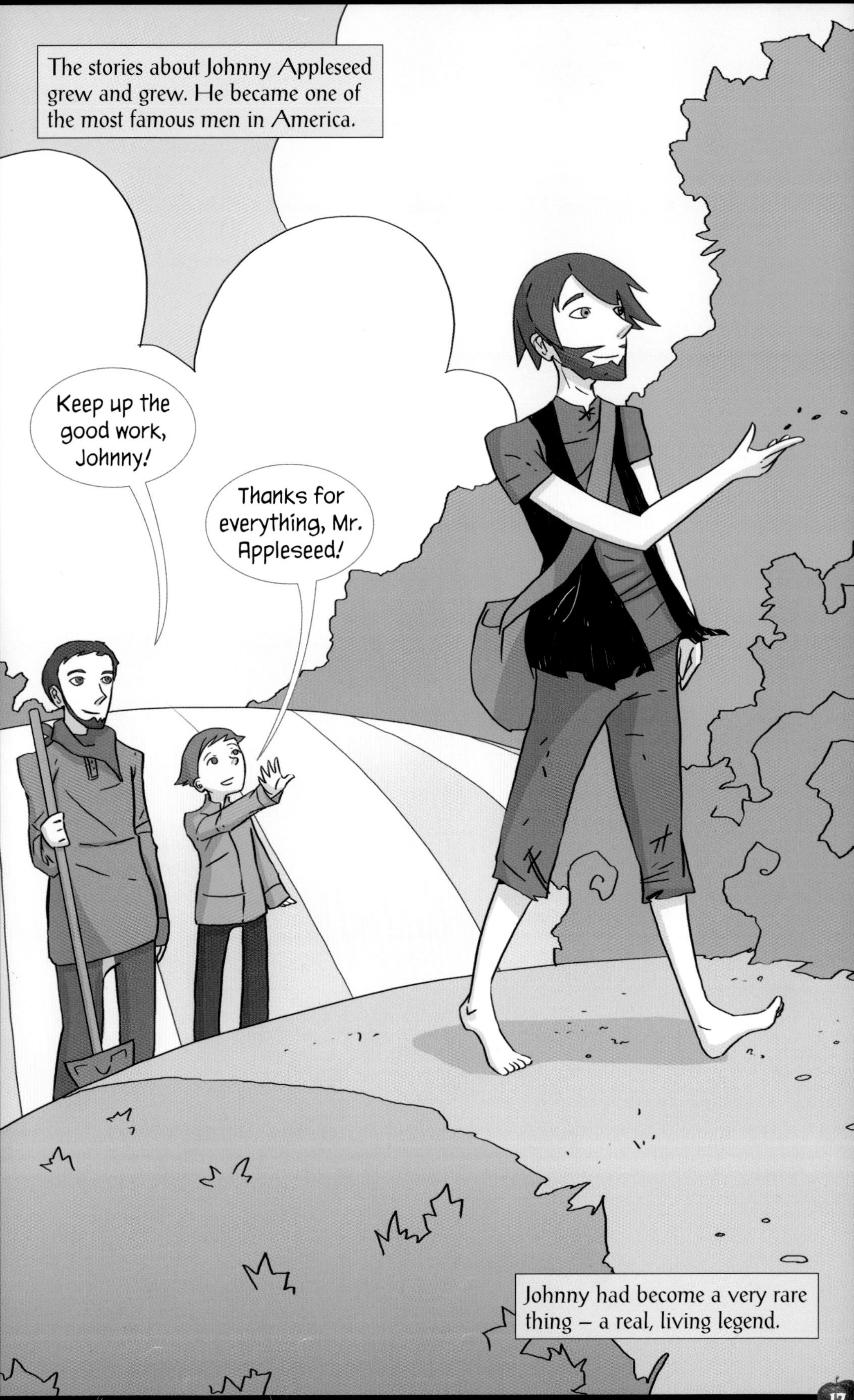
The stories about Johnny Appleseed grew and grew. He became one of the most famous men in America.
Keep up the good work, Johnny!
Thanks for everything, Mr. Appleseed!
Johnny had become a very rare thing – a real, living legend.

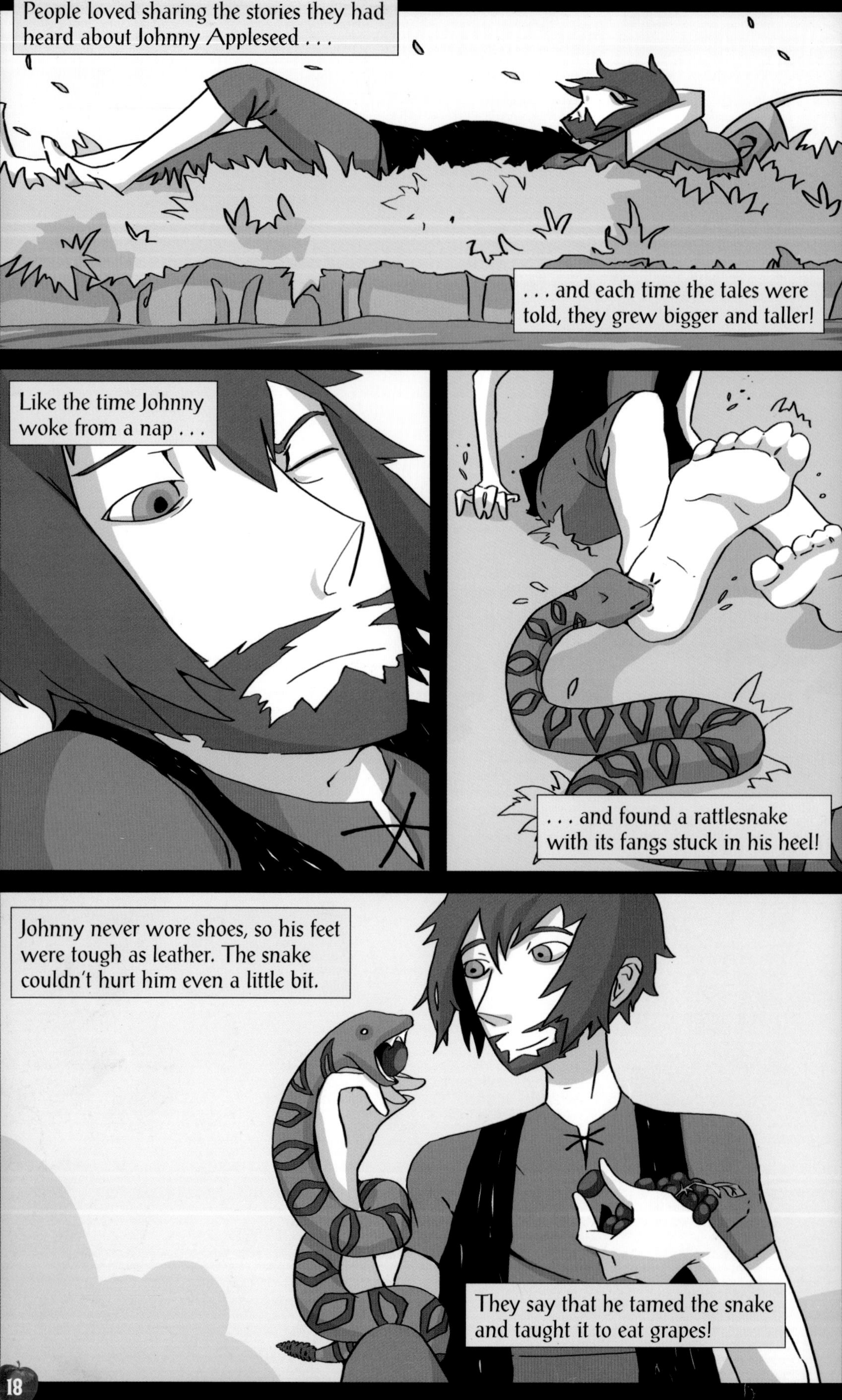
People loved sharing the stories they had heard about Johnny Appleseed . . .
. . . and each time the tales were told, they grew bigger and taller!
Like the time Johnny woke from a nap . . .
. . . and found a rattlesnake with its fangs stuck in his heel!
Johnny never wore shoes, so his feet were tough as leather. The snake couldn't hurt him even a little bit.
They say that he tamed the snake and taught it to eat grapes!

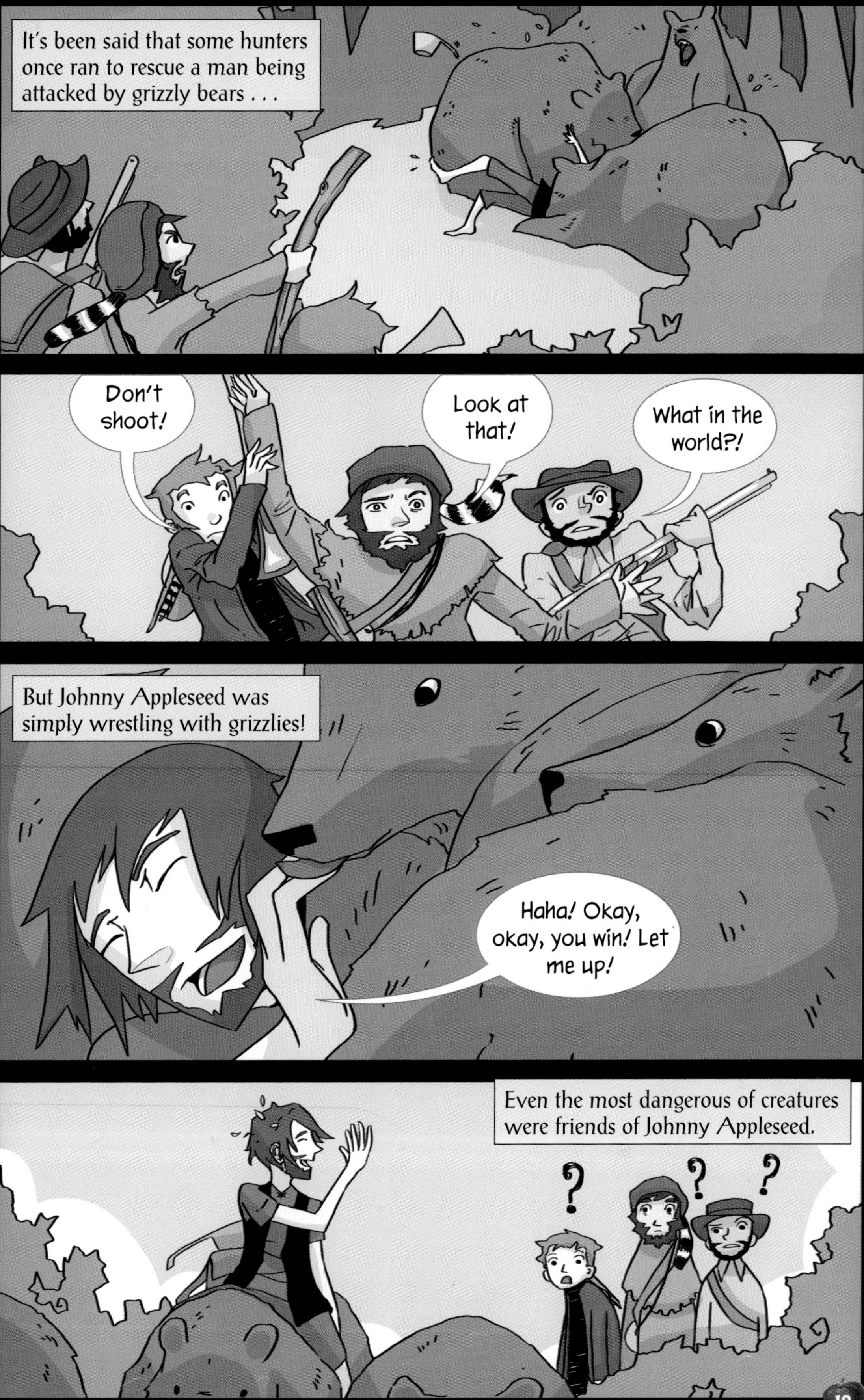
It's been said that some hunters once ran to rescue a man being attacked by grizzly bears . . .
Don't shoot!
Look at that!
What in the world?!
But Johnny Appleseed was simply wrestling with grizzlies!
Haha! Okay, okay, you win! Let me up!
Even the most dangerous of creatures were friends of Johnny Appleseed.
?
?
?

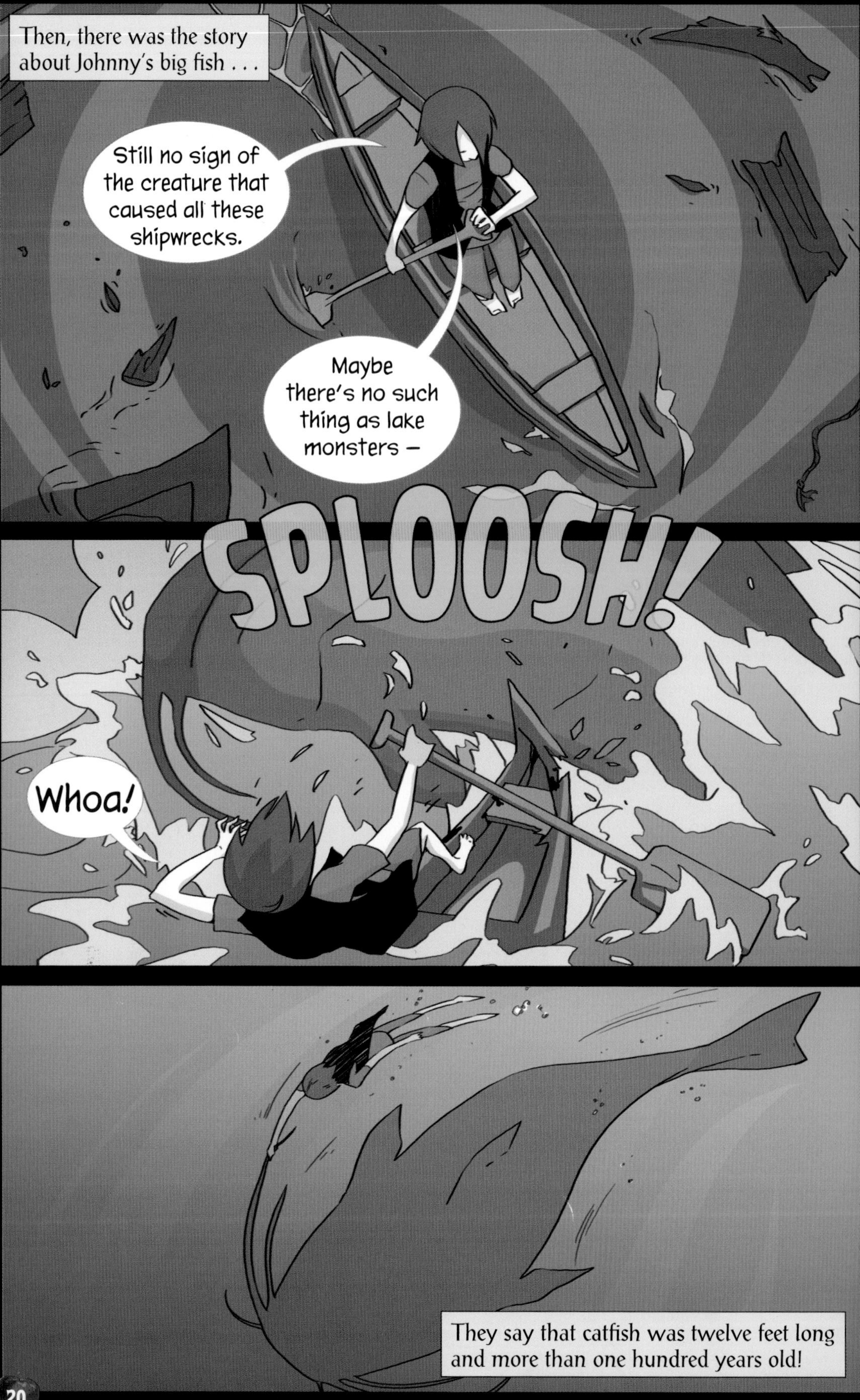
Then, there was the story about Johnny's big fish . . .
Still no sign of the creature that caused all these shipwrecks.
Maybe there's no such thing as lake monsters –
SPLOOSH!
Whoa!
They say that catfish was twelve feet long and more than one hundred years old!

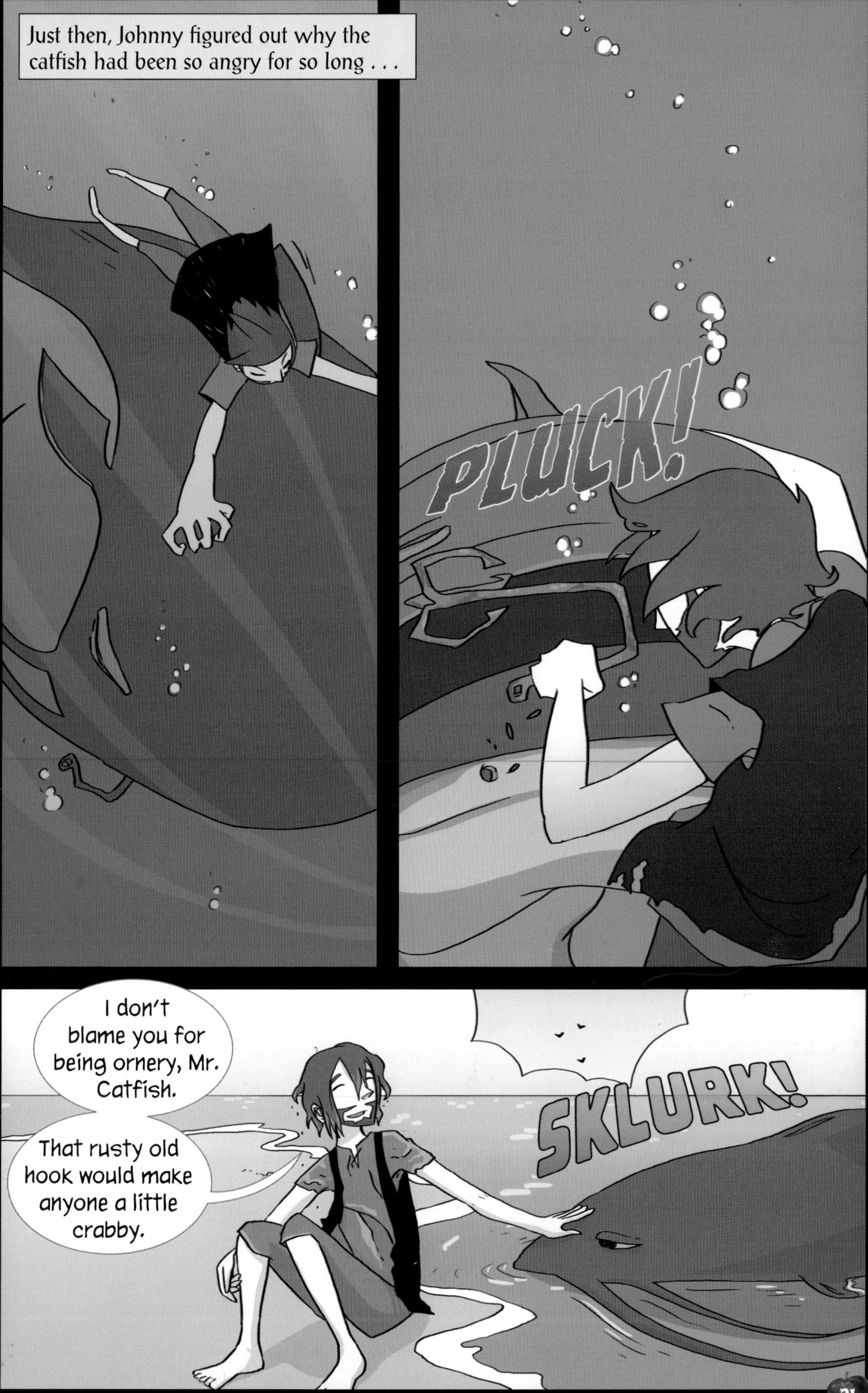
Just then, Johnny figured out why the catfish had been so angry for so long . . .
PLUCK!
I don't blame you for being ornery, Mr. Catfish.
That rusty old hook would make anyone a little crabby.
SKLURK!

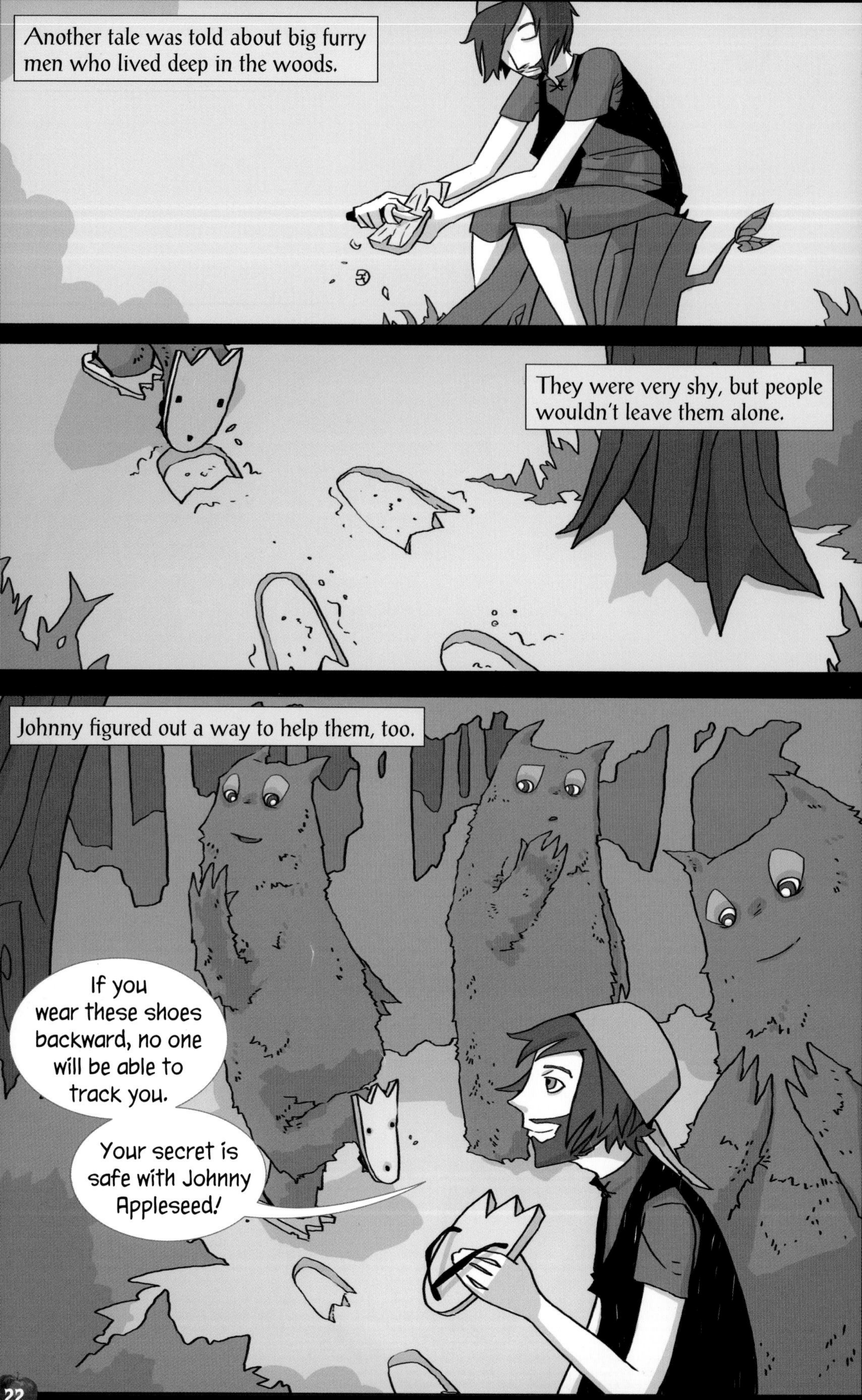
Another tale was told about big furry men who lived deep in the woods.
They were very shy, but people wouldn't leave them alone.
Johnny figured out a way to help them, too.
If you wear these shoes backward, no one will be able to track you.
Your secret is safe with Johnny Appleseed!

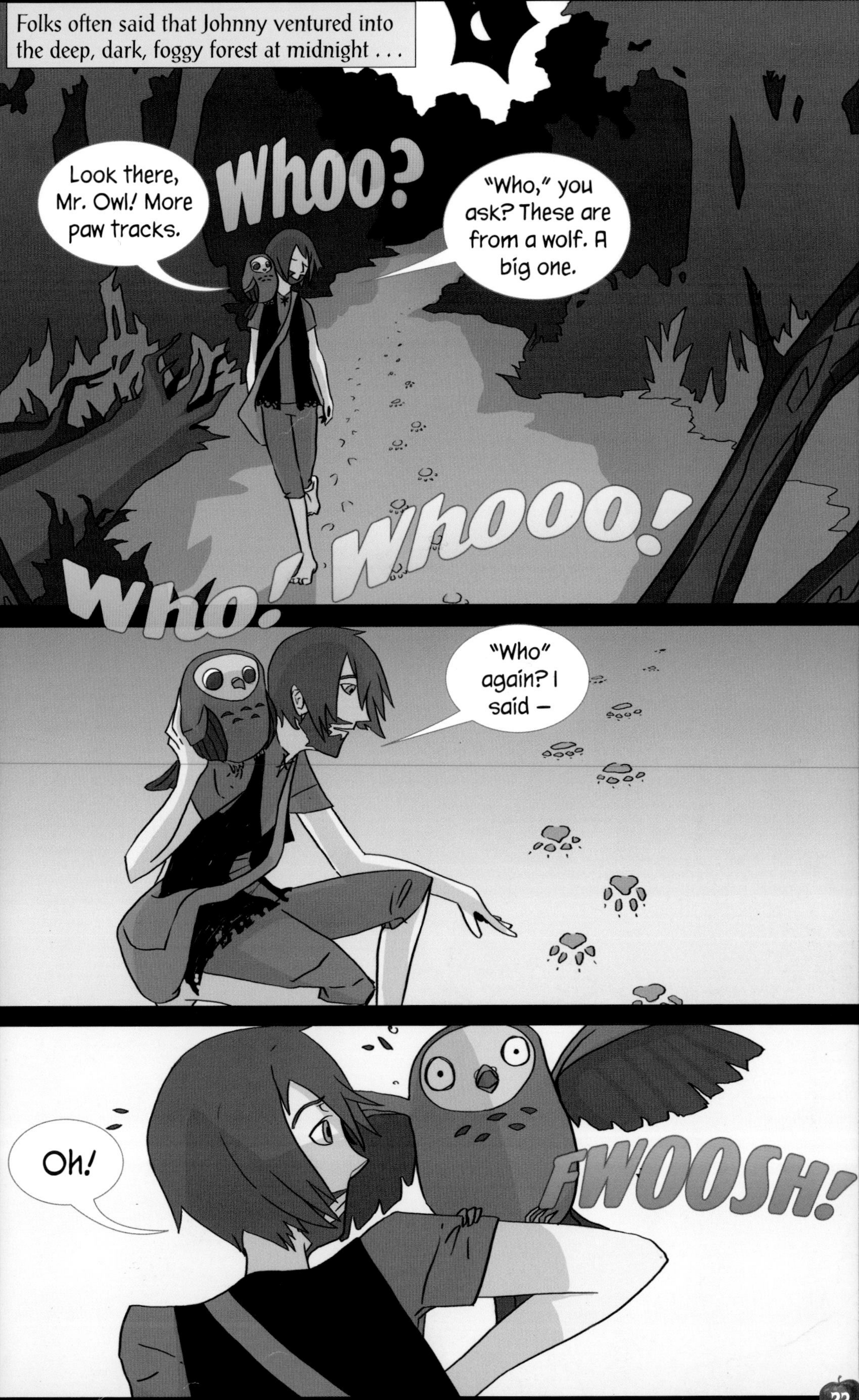
Folks often said that Johnny ventured into the deep, dark, foggy forest at midnight . . .
Look there, Mr. Owl! More paw tracks.
Whoo?
"Who," you ask? These are from a wolf. A big one.
Who! Whoooo!
"Who" again? I said –
Oh!
FWOOSH!

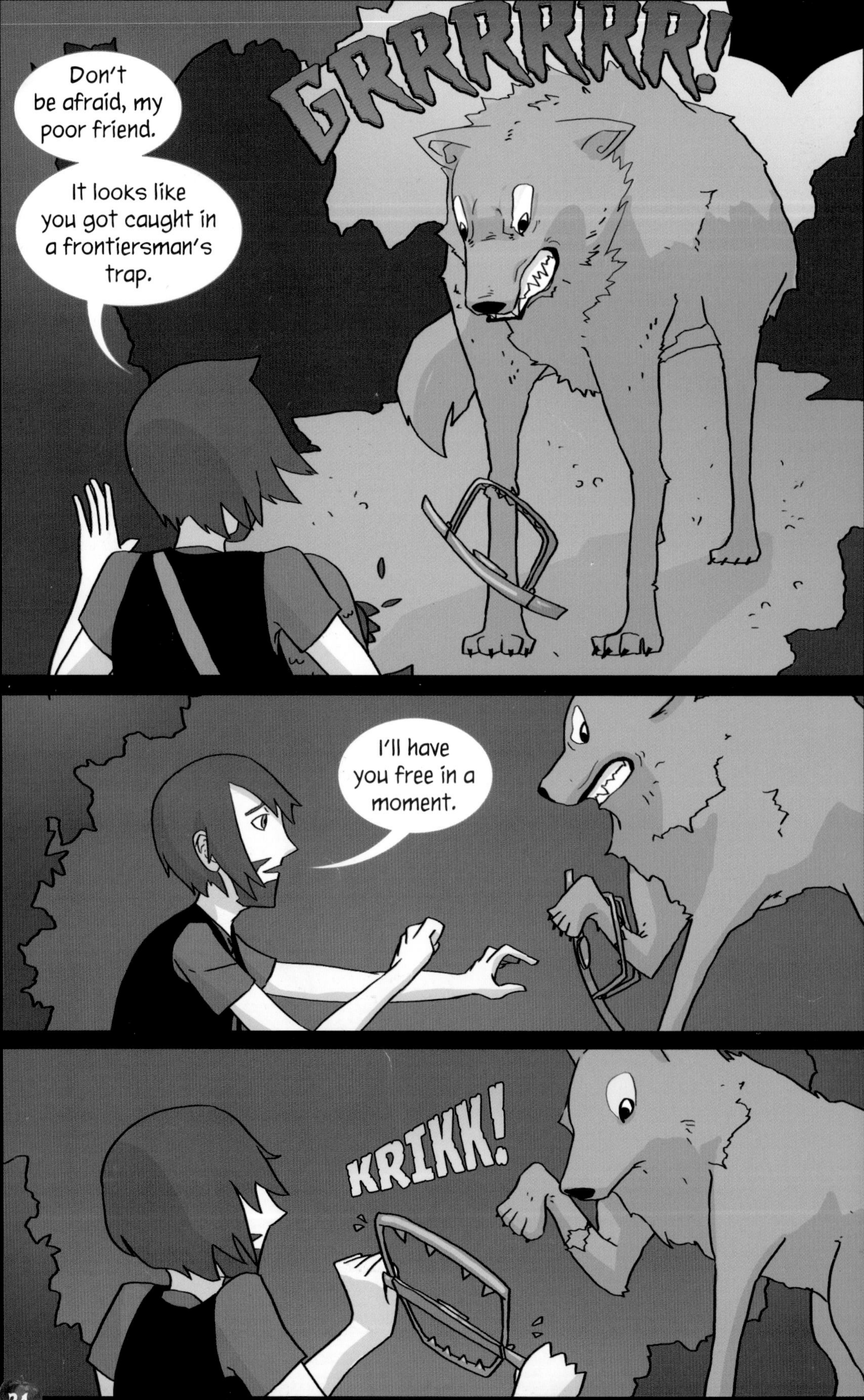
GRRRRRR!
Don't be afraid, my poor friend.
It looks like you got caught in a frontiersman's trap.
I'll have you free in a moment.
KRIKK!

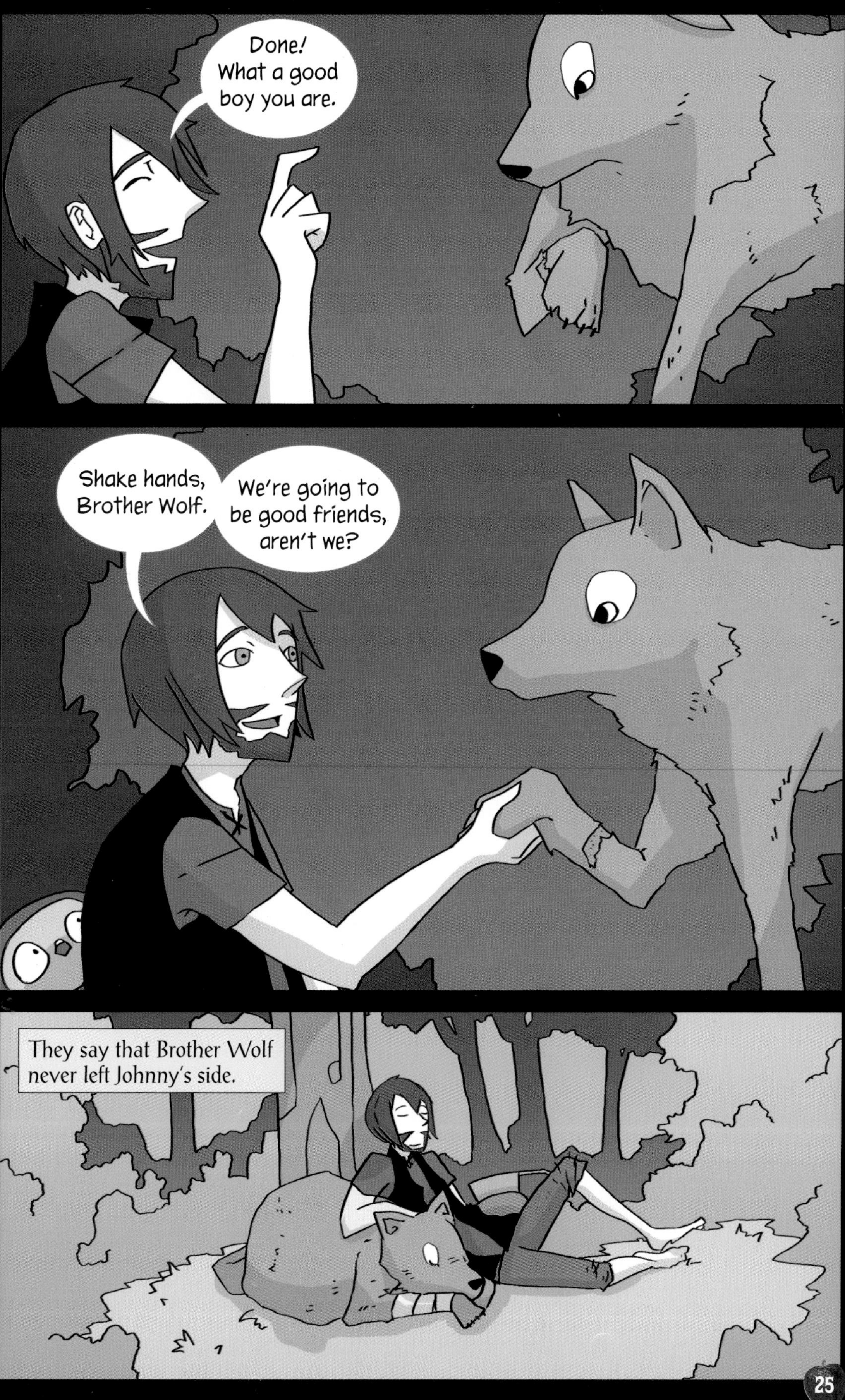
Done! What a good boy you are.
Shake hands, Brother Wolf.
We're going to be good friends, aren't we?
They say that Brother Wolf never left Johnny's side.

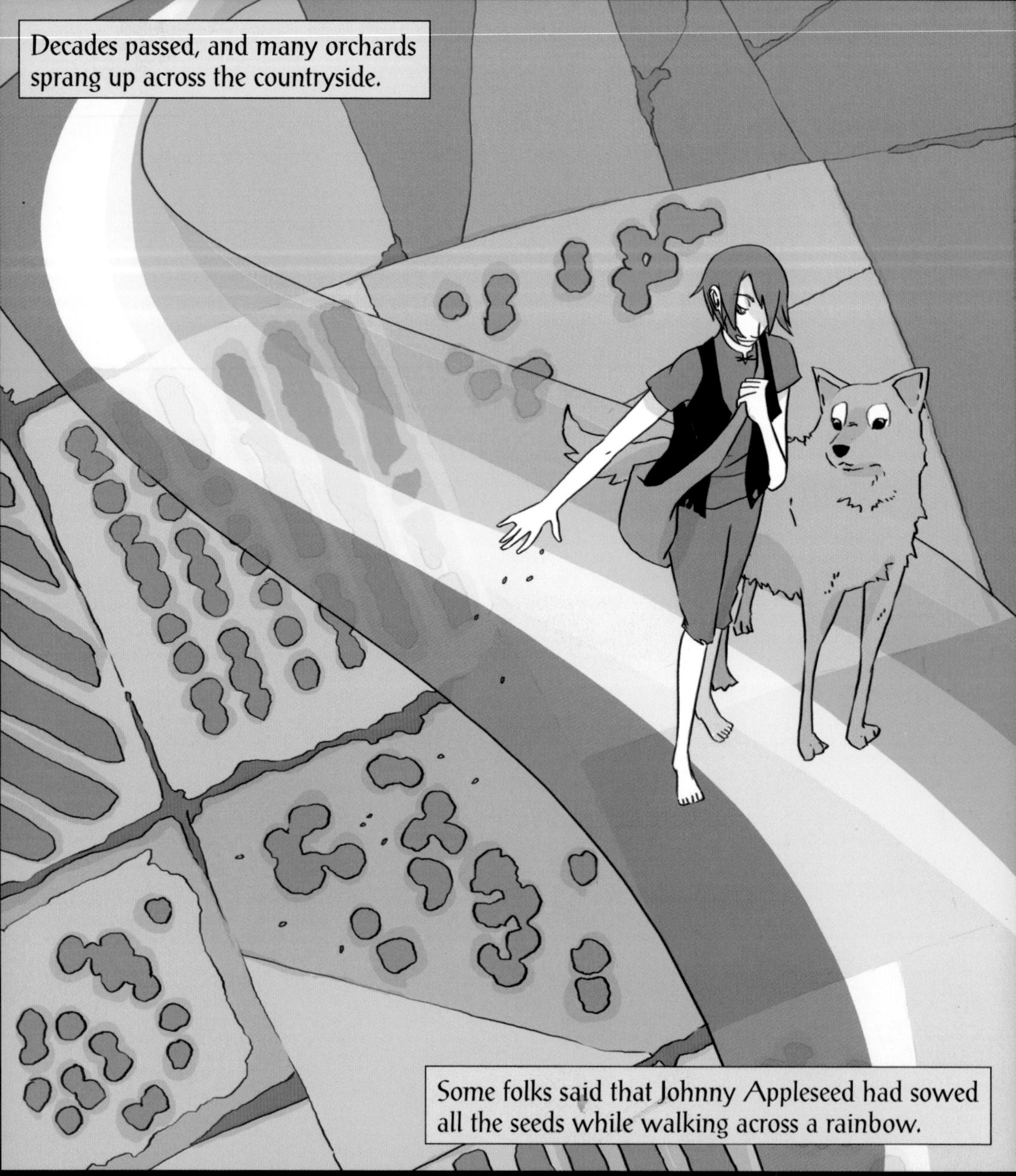
Decades passed, and many orchards sprang up across the countryside.
Some folks said that Johnny Appleseed had sowed all the seeds while walking across a rainbow.

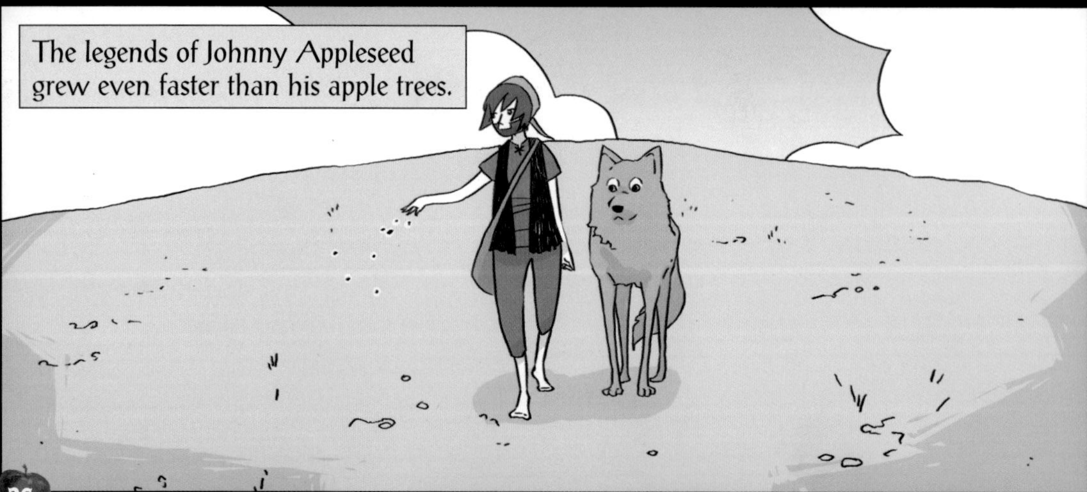
The legends of Johnny Appleseed grew even faster than his apple trees.

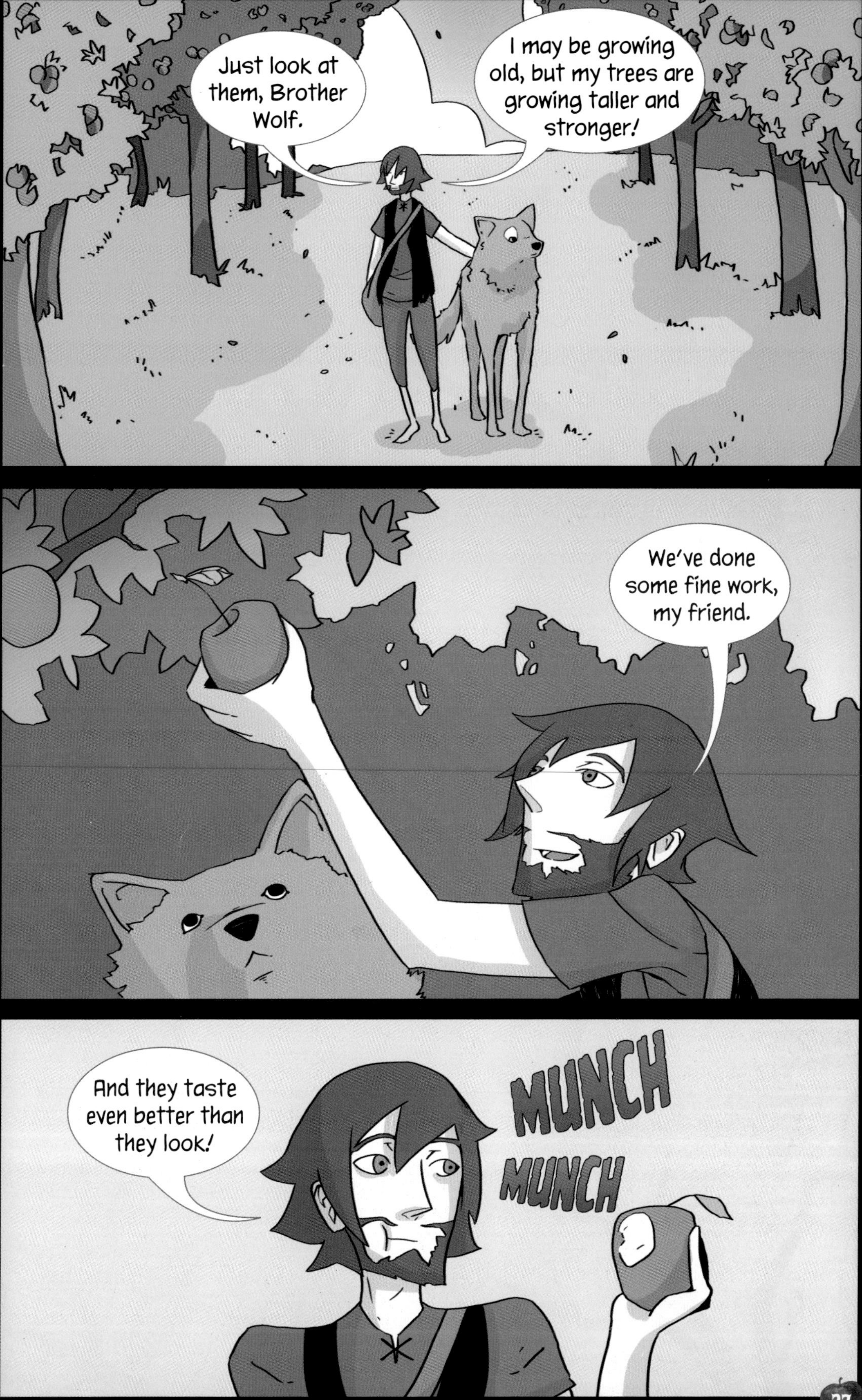

Just look at them, Brother Wolf.
I may be growing old, but my trees are growing taller and stronger!
We've done some fine work, my friend.
And they taste even better than they look!
MUNCH
MUNCH

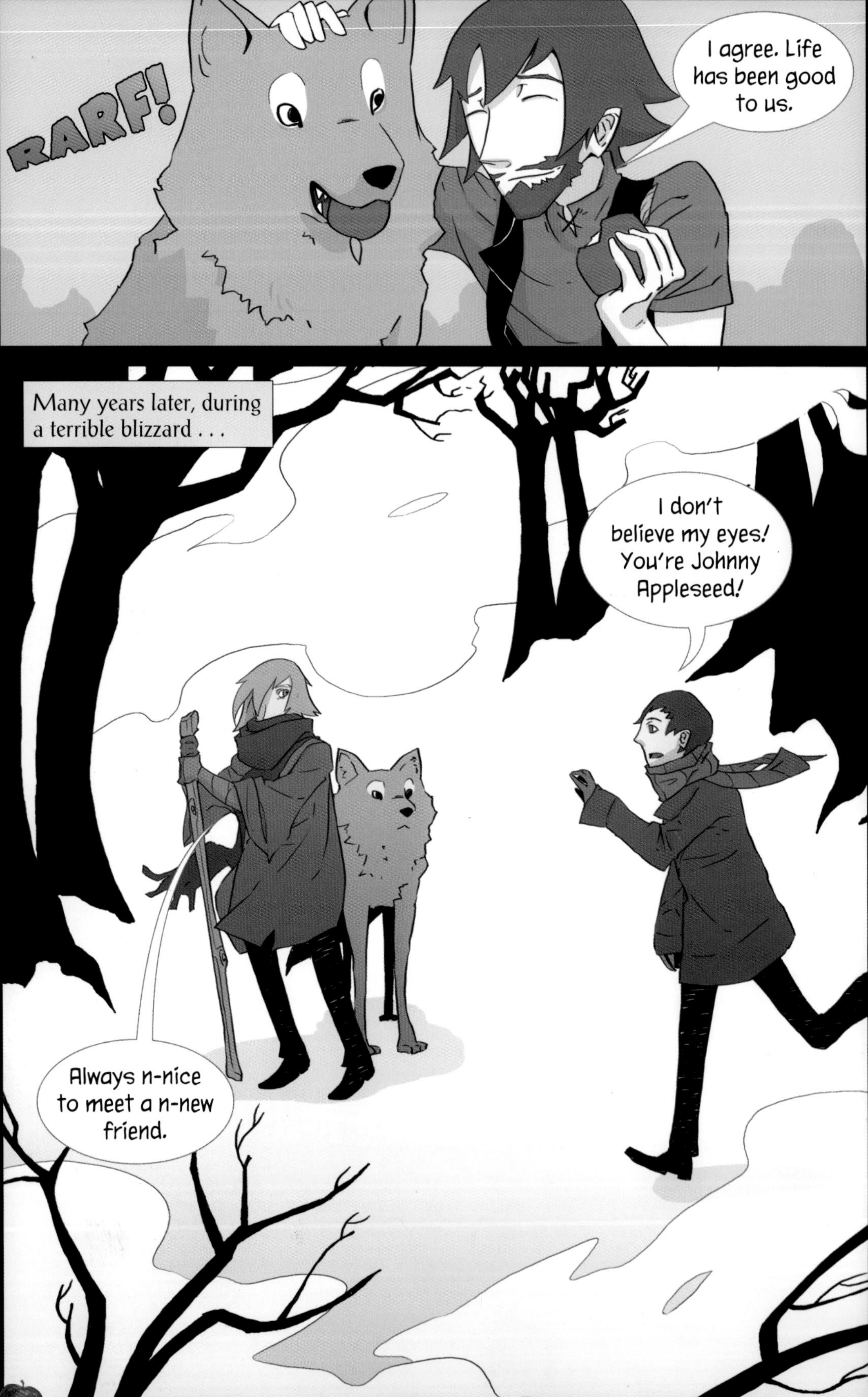
RARF!
I agree. Life has been good to us.
Many years later, during a terrible blizzard . . .
I don't believe my eyes! You're Johnny Appleseed!
Always n-nice to meet a n-new friend.

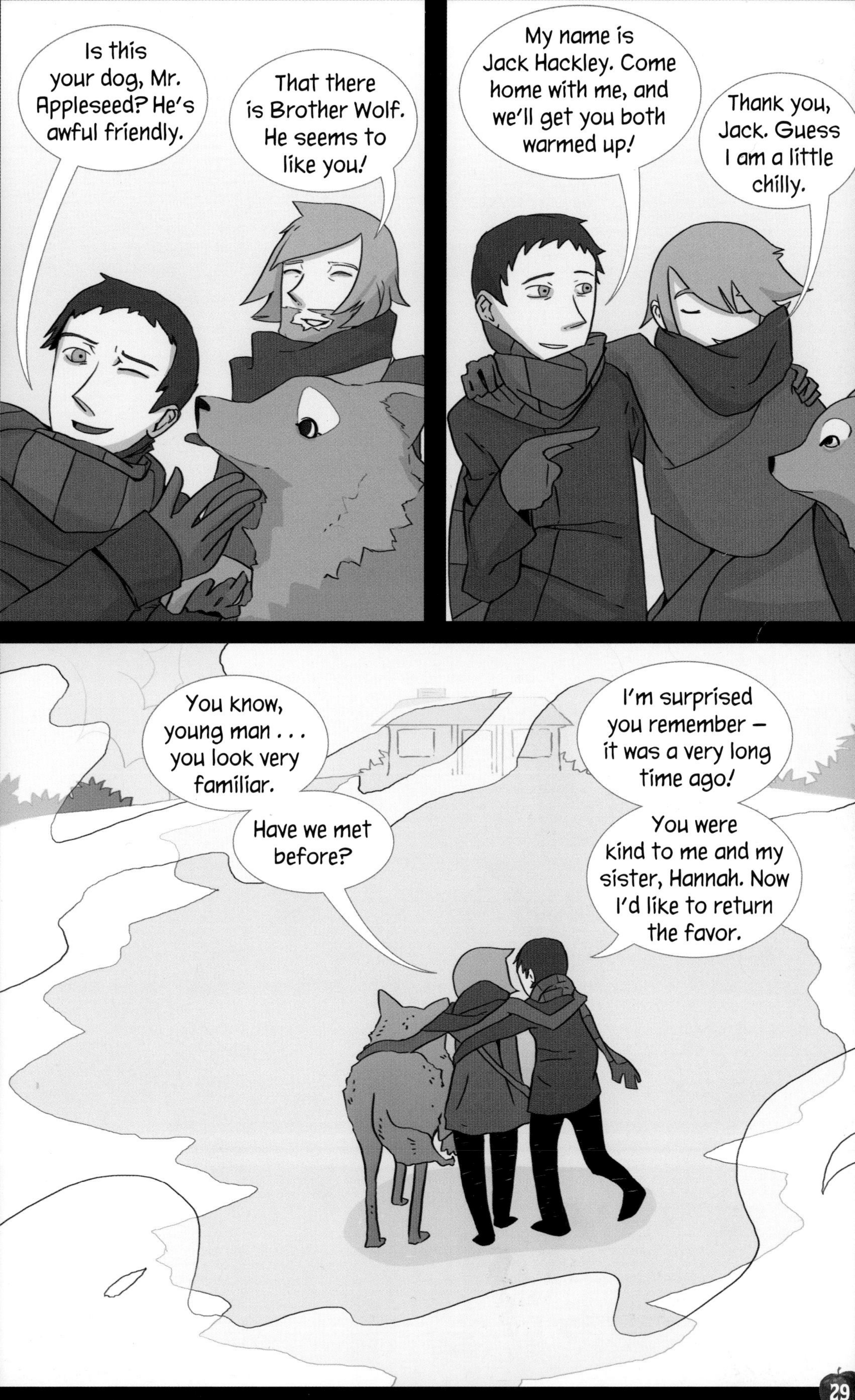
Is this your dog, Mr. Appleseed? He's awful friendly.
That there is Brother Wolf. He seems to like you!
My name is Jack Hackley. Come home with me, and we'll get you both warmed up!
Thank you, Jack. Guess I am a little chilly.
You know, young man . . . you look very familiar.
Have we met before?
I'm surprised you remember — it was a very long time ago!
You were kind to me and my sister, Hannah. Now I'd like to return the favor.

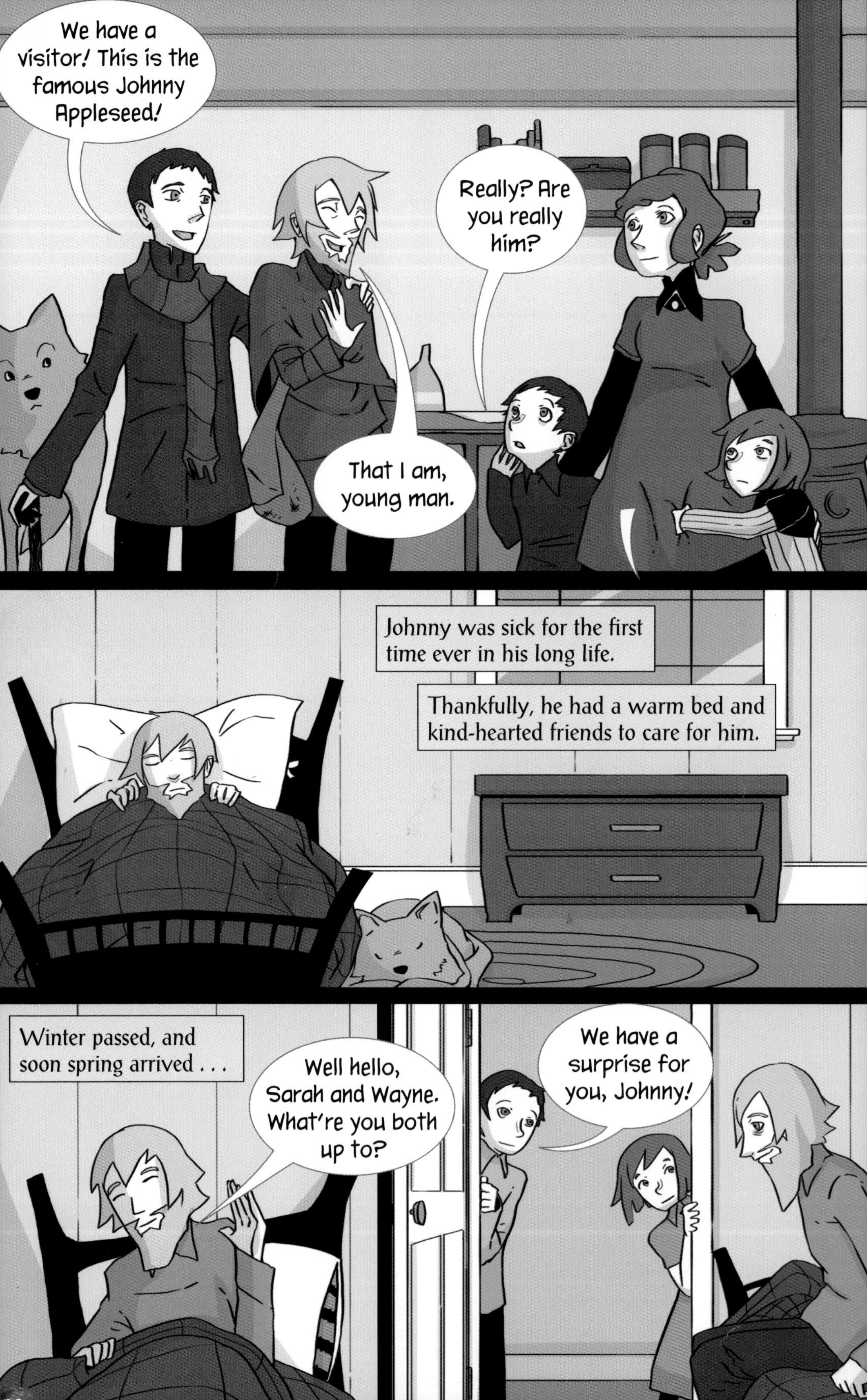
We have a visitor! This is the famous Johnny Appleseed!
Really? Are you really him?
That I am, young man.
Johnny was sick for the first time ever in his long life.
Thankfully, he had a warm bed and kind-hearted friends to care for him.
Winter passed, and soon spring arrived . . .
Well hello, Sarah and Wayne. What're you both up to?
We have a surprise for you, Johnny!

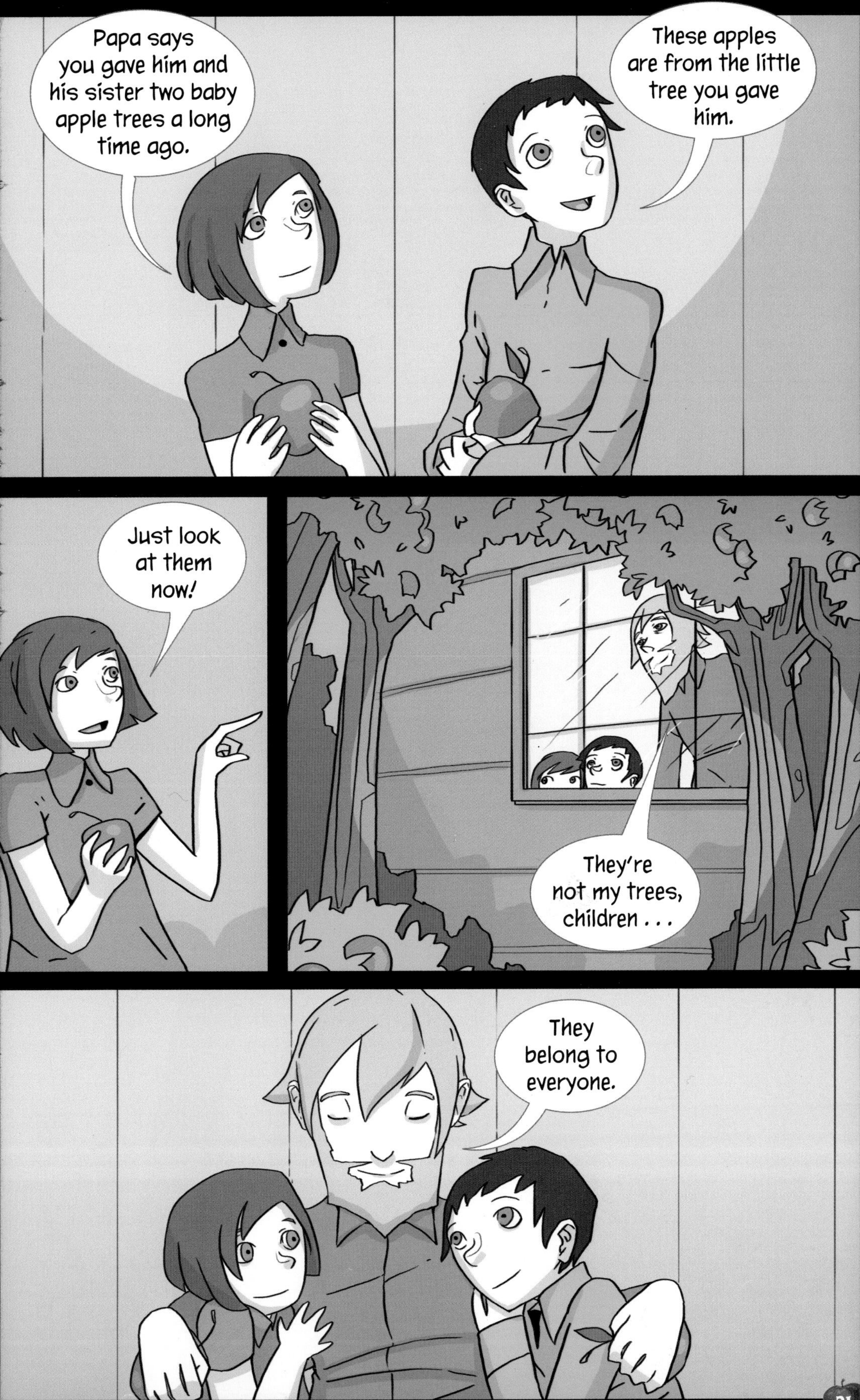
Papa says you gave him and his sister two baby apple trees a long time ago.
These apples are from the little tree you gave him.
Just look at them now!
They're not my trees, children . . .
They belong to everyone.

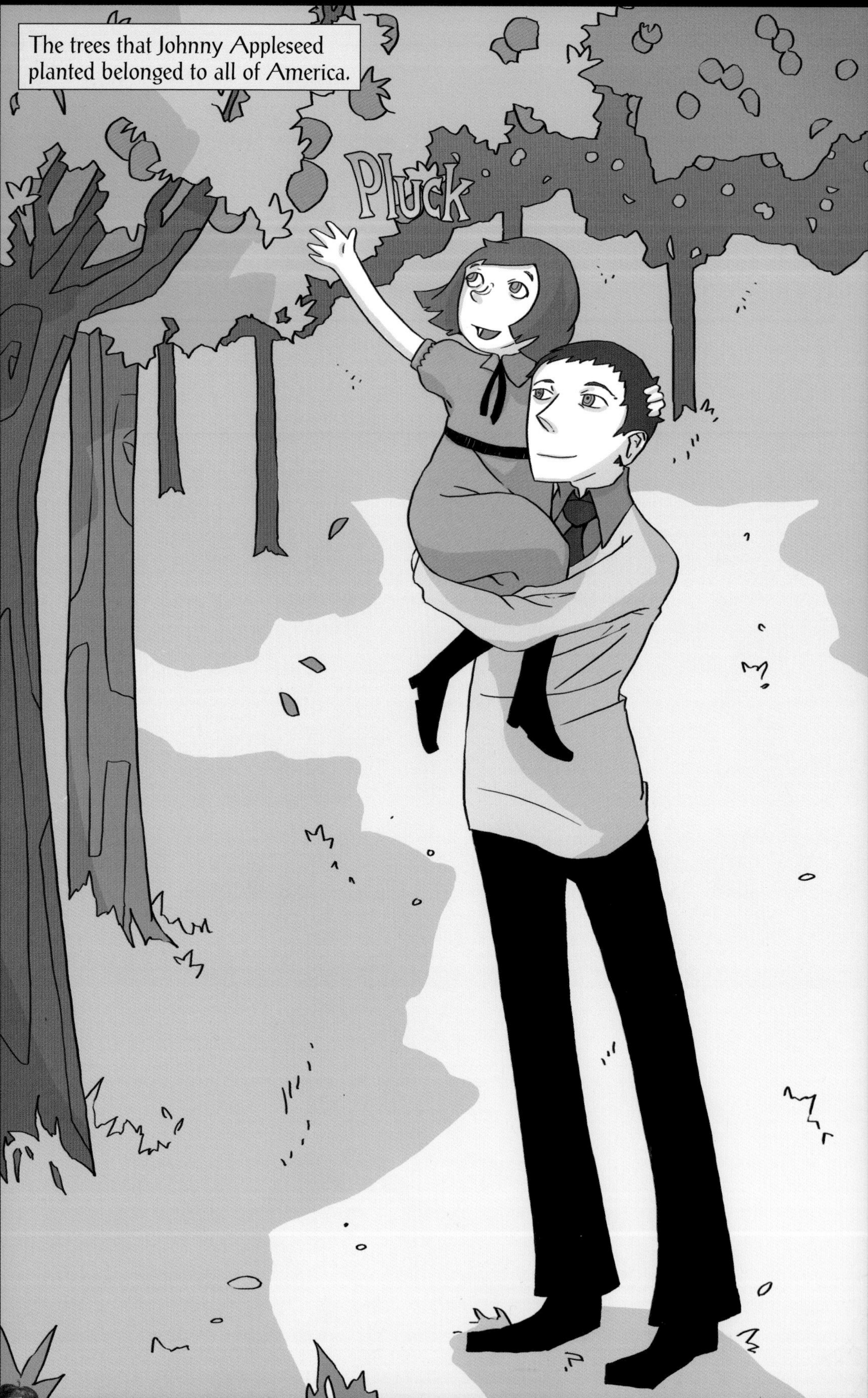
The trees that Johnny Appleseed planted belonged to all of America.
Pluck

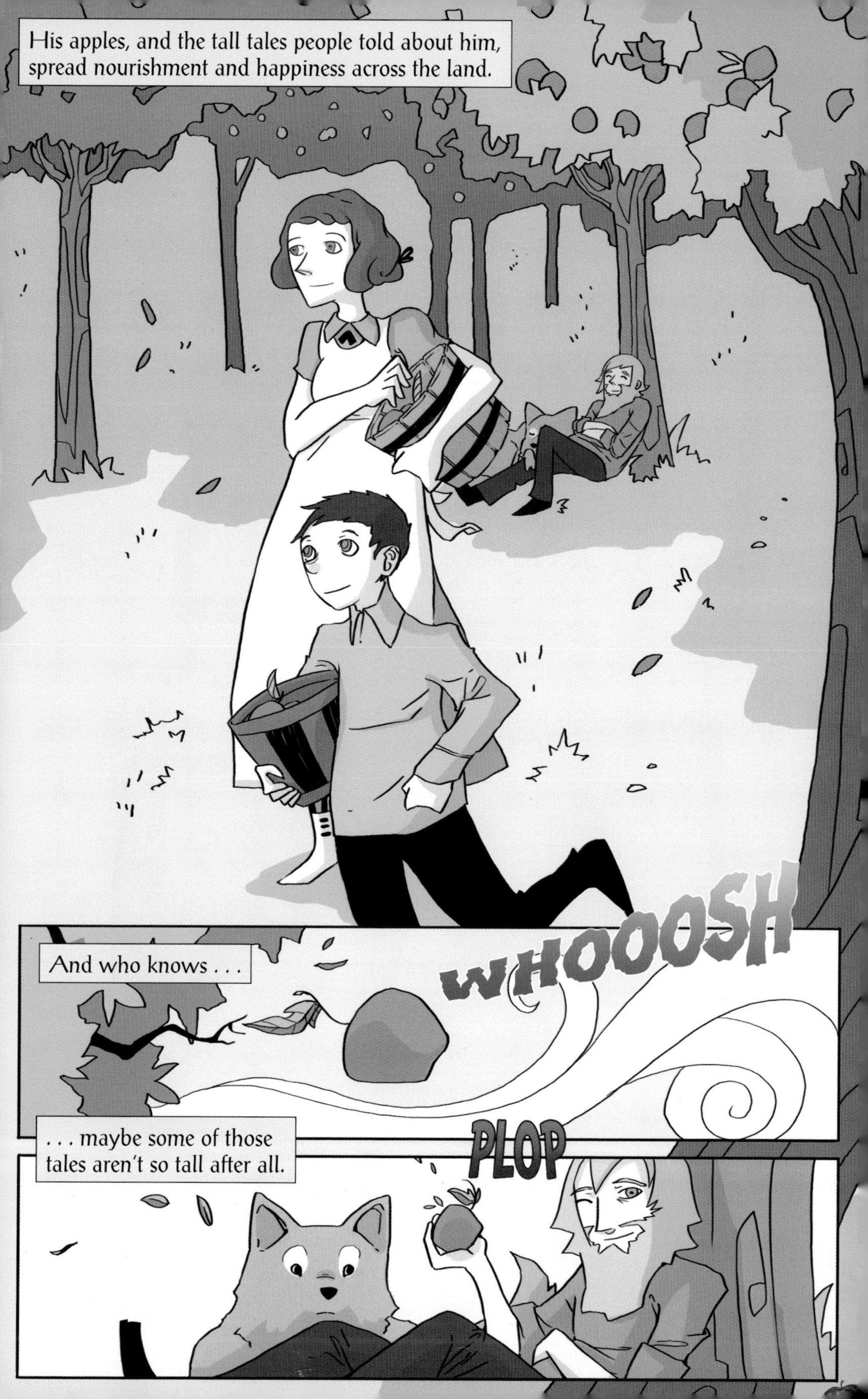

His apples, and the tall tales people told about him, spread nourishment and happiness across the land.
And who knows . . .
WHOOOSH
. . . maybe some of those tales aren't so tall after all.
PLOP

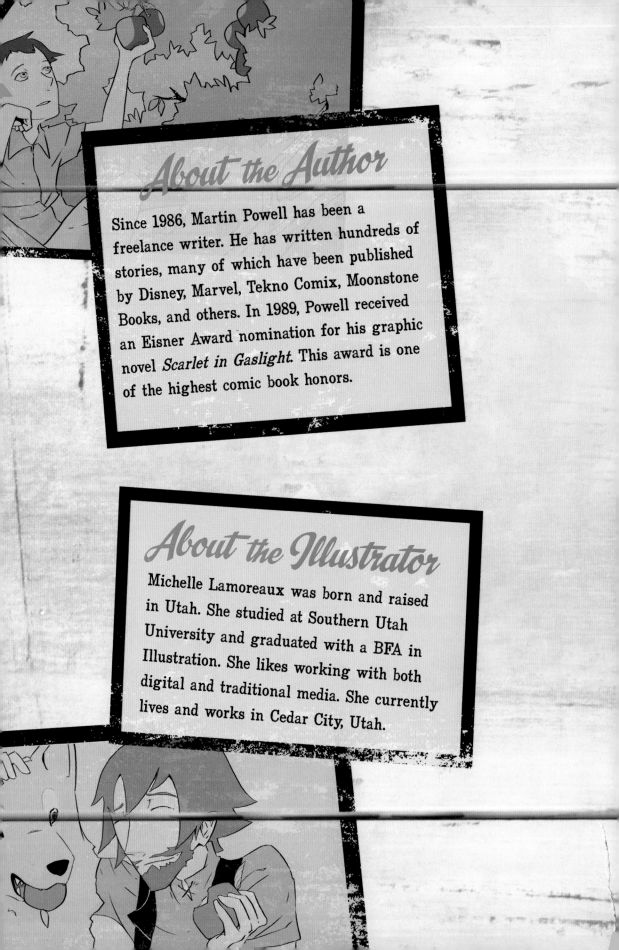

About the Author

Since 1986, Martin Powell has been a freelance writer. He has written hundreds of stories, many of which have been published by Disney, Marvel, Tekno Comix, Moonstone Books, and others. In 1989, Powell received an Eisner Award nomination for his graphic novel *Scarlet in Gaslight*. This award is one of the highest comic book honors.

About the Illustrator

Michelle Lamoreaux was born and raised in Utah. She studied at Southern Utah University and graduated with a BFA in Illustration. She likes working with both digital and traditional media. She currently lives and works in Cedar City, Utah.

Glossary

insist (in-SIST)—if you insist on something, you demand it very firmly

knack (NAK)—an ability to do something difficult or tricky

legend (LEJ-uhnd)—a story handed down from earlier times. Legends are often based on fact, but they are not entirely true.

nourishment (NUR-ish-ment)—if you give something nourishment, you give a person or animal enough food to keep him or her strong and healthy

orchards (OR-churdz)—fields or farms where fruit trees are grown

ornery (OR-nur-ee)—stubborn, mean, or agitated

pioneer (pye-uh-NEER)—one of the first people to work in a new and unknown area

sowed (SOHD)—planted, or scattered seeds over the ground so that they will grow

tamed (TAYMD)—taken from a wild or natural state and trained to live with or be useful to humans

ventured (VEN-churd)—put yourself at risk by doing something daring or dangerous

Johnny Appleseed
THE LIFE OF A LEGEND

Like his famous trees, the story of John Chapman started small, but grew into a real–life legend.

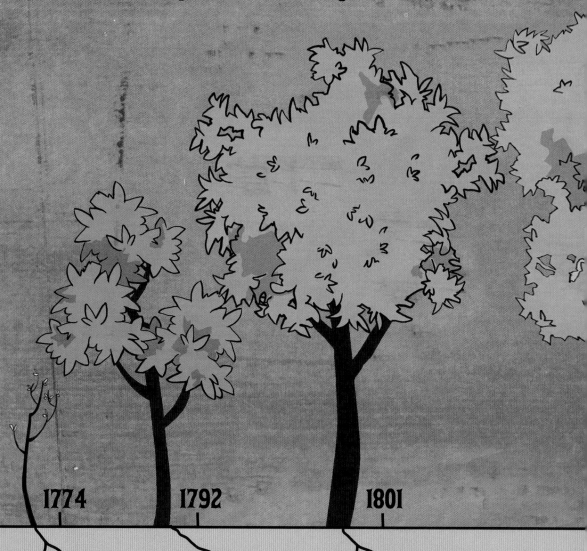

1774

1792

1801

On September 26, John Chapman, later known as Johnny Appleseed, is born in Leominster, Massachusetts, to Nathaniel and Elizabeth Chapman.

The 18–year–old Chapman travels west, taking his 11–year–old brother, Nathaniel, and his sister, Elizabeth, with him.

Chapman transports 16 bushels, or about 8 gallons, of apple seeds down the Ohio River. He collected the seeds from cider presses along his travels, and planted them on his way.

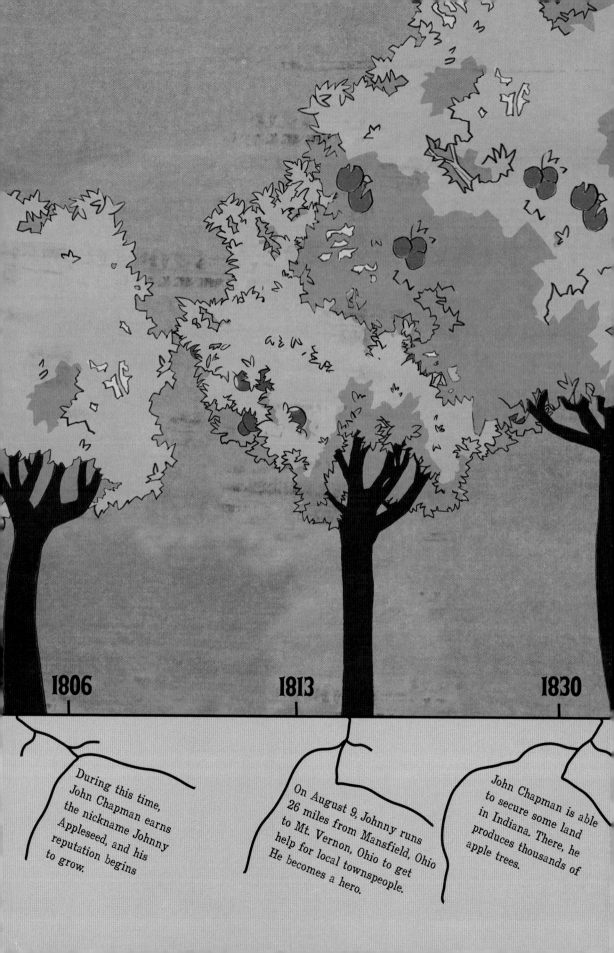

1806

1813

1830

During this time, John Chapman earns the nickname Johnny Appleseed, and his reputation begins to grow.

On August 9, Johnny runs 26 miles from Mansfield, Ohio to Mt. Vernon, Ohio to get help for local townspeople. He becomes a hero.

John Chapman is able to secure some land in Indiana. There, he produces thousands of apple trees.

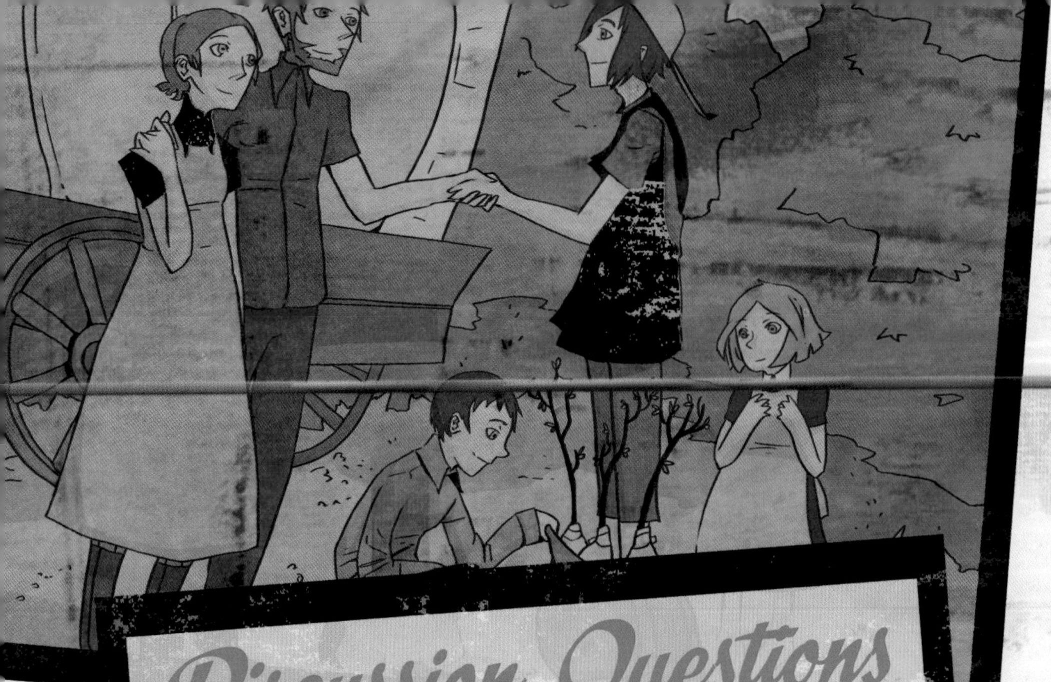

Discussion Questions

1. John Chapman was given the nickname Johnny Appleseed because he loved apples. If you were named after your favorite food, what would your nickname be?
2. Tall tales tell stories about real-life things, but they are usually very exaggerated. What parts of this tall tale could have been true?
3. Johnny helped both the American Indians and the pioneers even though they were at war with each other. Should you always take sides in an argument or fight? Why or why not?

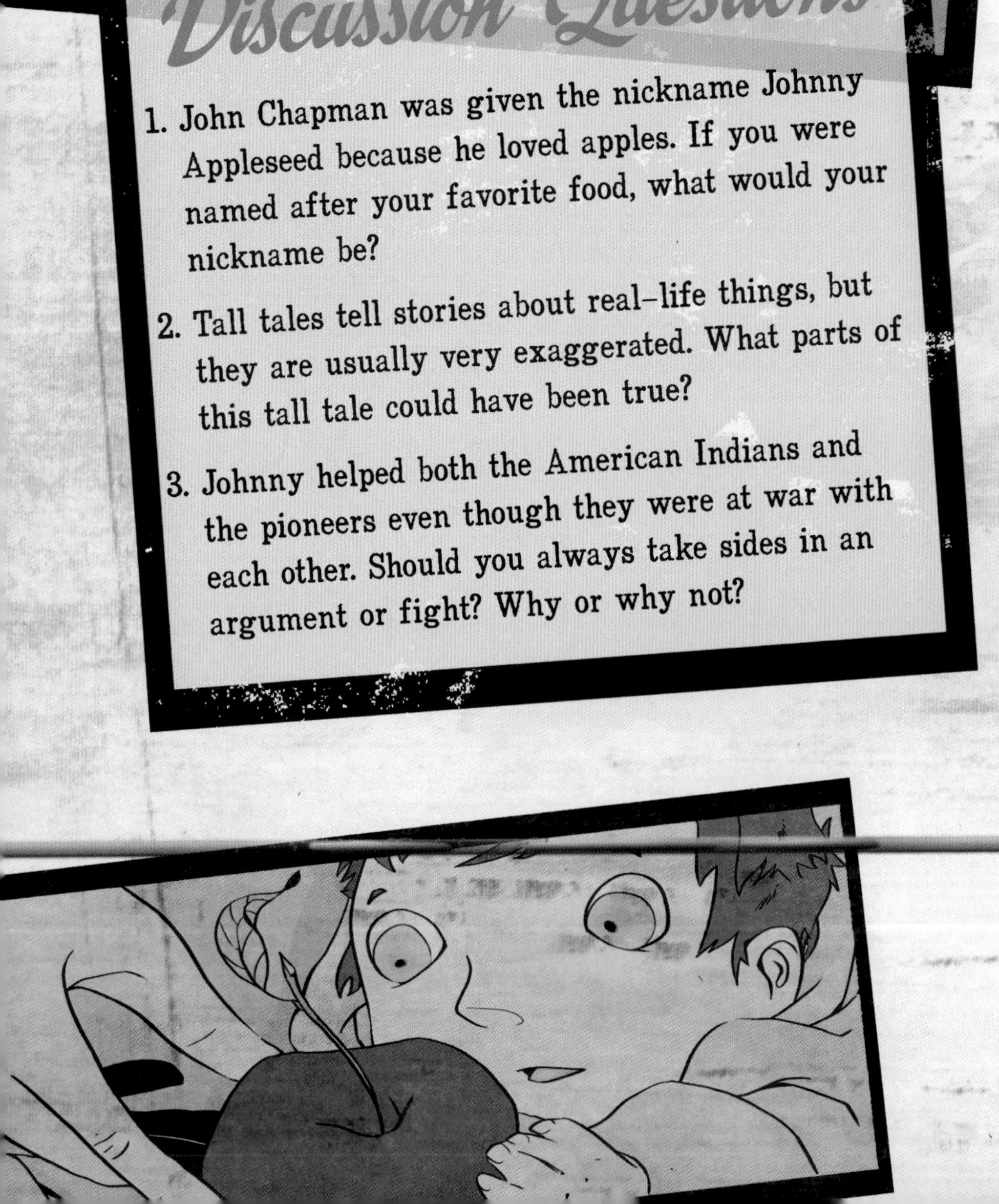

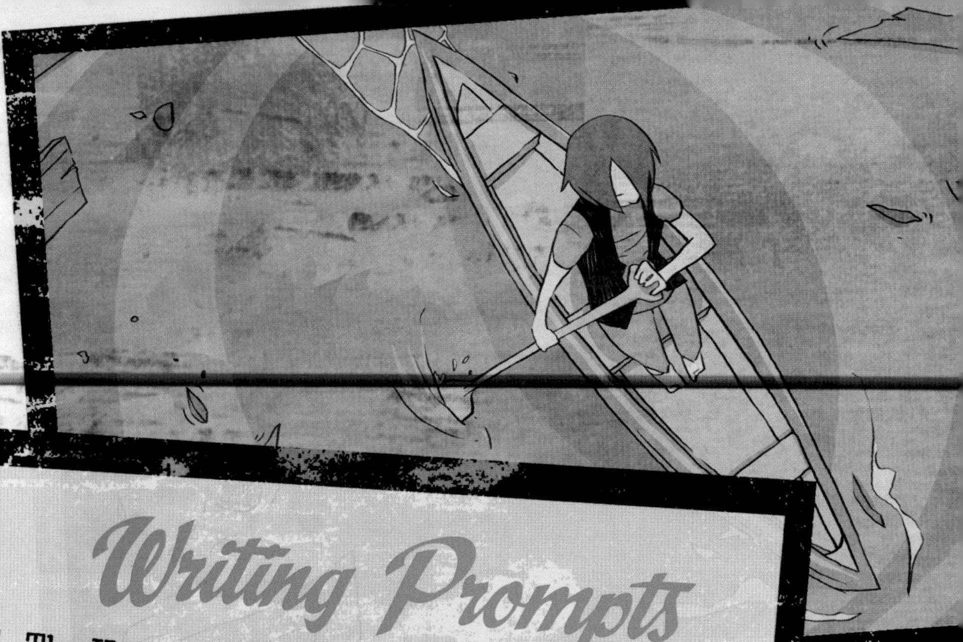

Writing Prompts

1. The Hackley family lets Johnny stay with them when he's sick and cold. Has anyone ever helped you during a difficult time? Who have you helped when things were tough? Write about your helpful experiences.
2. Johnny saves Brother Wolf, and the two become friends. If you could have any kind of wild animal as a pet, what would it be? Write about your dream pet. Then draw a picture of it.
3. Johnny Appleseed tried very hard to live a good and honest life. What kind of life do you want to live? Do you want to do good, help others, experience adventures, or just have fun?

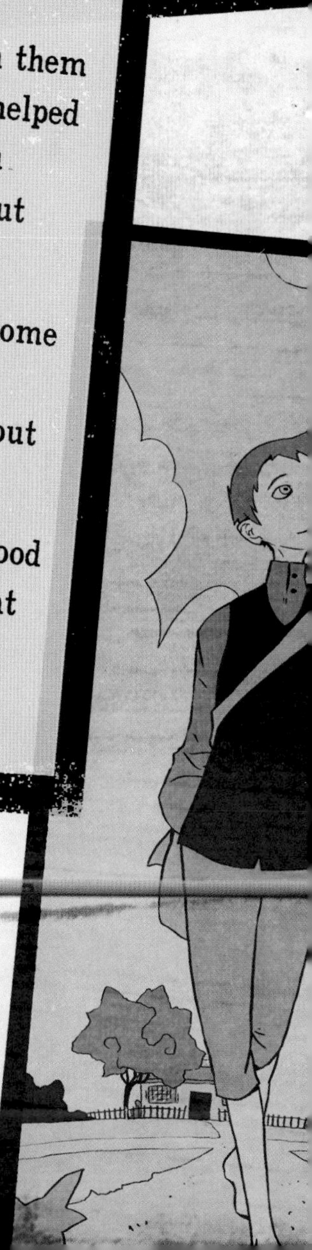

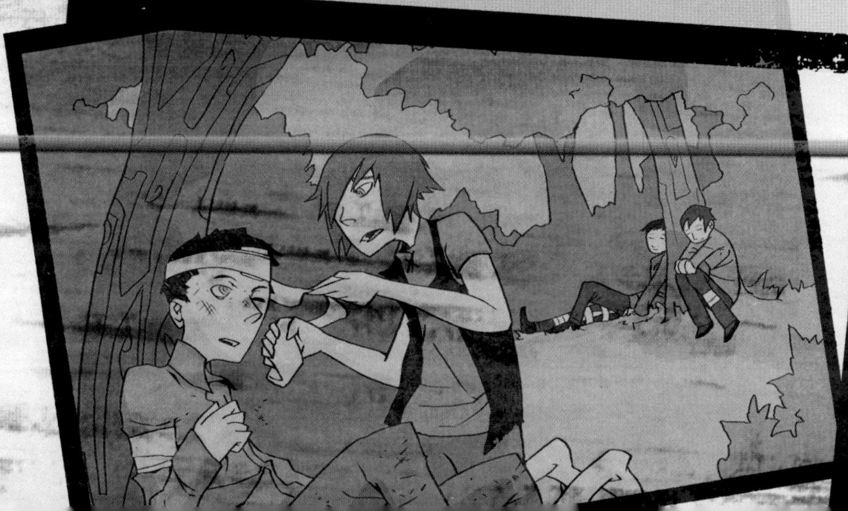

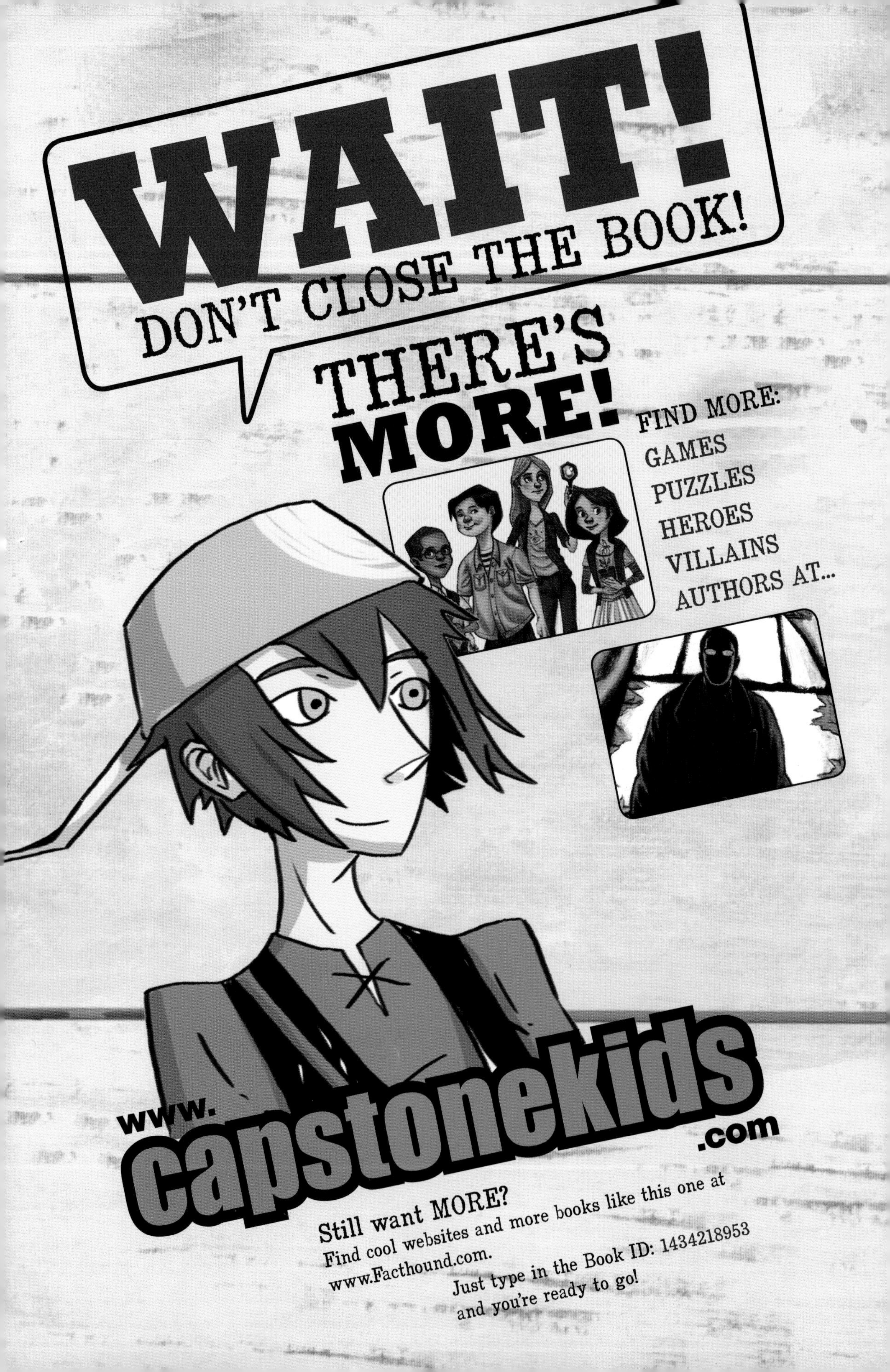
WAIT!
DON'T CLOSE THE BOOK!
THERE'S MORE!
FIND MORE:
GAMES
PUZZLES
HEROES
VILLAINS
AUTHORS AT...
www.capstonekids.com
Still want MORE?
Find cool websites and more books like this one at www.Facthound.com.
Just type in the Book ID: 1434218953
and you're ready to go!